CL

St. Helens Libraries

Please return / renew this item by the last date shown.
Books may be renewed by phone and Internet.

Telephone - (01744) 676954 or 677822
Email - centrallibrary@sthelens.gov.uk
Online - sthelens.gov.uk/librarycatalogue
Twitter - twitter.com/STHLibraries
Facebook - facebook.com/STHLibraries

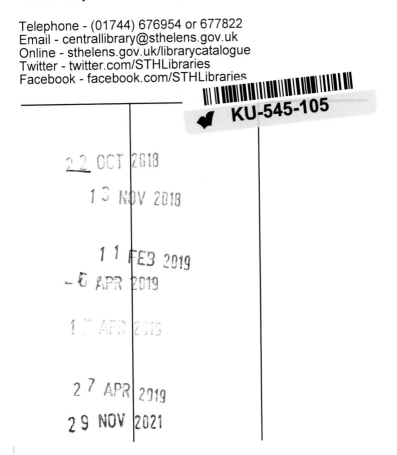

CASTIGLIONE'S
PREGNANT
PRINCESS

CASTIGLIONE'S PREGNANT PRINCESS

LYNNE GRAHAM

MILLS & BOON

First published in Great Britain 2018
by Mills & Boon, an imprint of HarperCollins*Publishers*
1 London Bridge Street, London, SE1 9GF

Large Print edition 2018

© 2018 Lynne Graham

ISBN: 978-0-263-07397-3

MIX
Paper from
responsible sources
FSC® C007454

This book is produced from independently certified FSC™ paper to ensure responsible forest management. For more information visit www.harpercollins.co.uk/green.

Printed and bound in Great Britain
by CPI Group (UK) Ltd, Croydon, CR0 4YY

CHAPTER ONE

'COME ON,' ZAC DA ROCHA chided his brother. 'There's got to be some room for manoeuvre here, something that you want more than that car. Sell it to me and I'll buy you anything you want.'

Fierce hostility roared through Prince Vitale Castiglione because his Brazilian half-brother irritated the hell out of him. The fact that they were both luxury-car collectors had to be the only thing they had in common. But no didn't ever mean no to Zac; no only made Zac raise the price. He couldn't seem to grasp the reality that Vitale couldn't be bribed. But then, Zacarias Da Rocha, heir to the fabled Quintel Da Rocha diamond mines and fabulously wealthy even by his brothers' standards, was unaccustomed to refusal or disappointment and constitutionally incapable of respecting polite boundaries. His lean, strong face grim, Vitale shot a glance at the younger man, his brilliant dark eyes impassive with years of hard self-discipline.

'No,' Vitale repeated quietly, wishing his older brother, Angel Valtinos, would return and shut Zac up because being rude didn't come naturally to Vitale, who had been raised in the stifling traditions and formality of a European royal family. A lifetime of rigid conditioning invariably stepped in to prevent Vitale from losing his temper and revealing his true feelings.

Of course, it had already been a most unsettling morning. Vitale had been disconcerted when his father, Charles Russell, had asked both him and his two brothers to meet him at his office. It had been an unusual request because Charles usually made the effort to meet his sons separately and Vitale had wondered if some sort of family emergency had occurred until Charles had appeared and swept his eldest son, Angel, off into his office alone, leaving Vitale with only Zac for company. Not a fun development that, Vitale reflected before studiously telling himself off for that negative outlook.

After all, it wasn't Zac's fault that he had only met his father the year before and was still very much a stranger to his half-brothers, who, in spite of their respective parents' divorces, had known each other since early childhood. Unhappily, Zac with his untamed black hair, tattoos and aggressive attitude simply didn't fit in. He was too unconventional, too competitive, too *much* in every way. Nor did it help that he was only a couple of months younger than Vitale, which underlined the reality that Zac had been conceived while Charles Russell had still been married to Vitale's mother. Yet Vitale could understand how that adulterous affair had come about. His mother was cold while his father was emotional and caring. He suspected that while caught up in the divorce that had devastated him Charles had sought comfort from a warmer woman.

'Then let's make a bet,' Zac suggested irrepressibly.

Vitale was tempted to roll his eyes in comic disbelief but he said nothing.

'I heard you and Angel talking earlier about the big palace ball being held in Lerovia at the end of next month,' Zac admitted softly. 'I understand that it's a very formal, upmarket occasion and that your mother is expecting you to pick a wife from her selection of carefully handpicked female guests...'

Faint colour illuminated Vitale's rigid high cheekbones and he ground his even white teeth. 'Queen Sofia enjoys trying to organise my life but I have no current plans to marry.'

'But it would be a hell of a lot easier to keep all those women at bay if you turned up with a partner of your own,' Zac pointed out without skipping a beat, as if he knew by some mysterious osmosis how much pressure Vitale's royal parent invariably put on her only child's shoulders. 'So, this is the bet... I bet you that you couldn't transform an ordinary woman into a convincing socialite for the evening and pass her off as the real thing. If you manage that feat, I'll give you my rarest vehicle but naturally I'll expect an invitation to the ball. If your lady fails the test, you hand over your most precious car.'

Vitale almost rolled his eyes at that outrageously juvenile challenge. Obviously he didn't do bets. He raked his black glossy hair back from his brow in a gesture of impatience. 'I'm not Pygmalion and I don't know any *ordinary* women,' he admitted truthfully.

'Who's Pygmalion?' Zac asked with a genuine frown. 'And how can you not know any ordinary women? You live in the same world I do.'

'Not quite.' Vitale's affairs were always very discreet and he avoided the sort of tacky, celebrity-chasing women likely to boast of him as a conquest, while Zac seemed to view any attractive woman as fair game. Vitale, however, didn't want to run the risk of any tabloid exposés containing the kind of sexual revelations that would dishonour the Lerovian throne.

In addition, he was an investment banker and CEO of the very conservative and respectable Bank of Lerovia, thus expected to live a very staid life: bankers who led rackety lives made investors unprofitably nervous. Lerovia was, after all, a tax shelter of international repute. It was a small country, hemmed in by much larger, more powerful countries, and Vitale's grandfather had built Lerovia's wealth and stability on a secure financial base. Vitale had had few career options open to him. His mother had wanted him to simply be the Crown Prince, her heir in waiting, but Vitale had needed a greater purpose, not to mention the freedom to become a man in his own right, something his autocratic mother would never have willingly given him.

He had fought for his right to have a career just as he now fought for his continuing freedom of choice as a single man. At only twenty-eight, he wasn't ready for the responsibility of a wife or, even more depressingly, the demands of a baby. His stomach sank at the prospect of a crying, clinging child looking to him for support. He also knew better than anyone how difficult it would be for any woman to enter the Lerovian royal family and be forced to deal with his domineering mother, the current Queen. His unfortunate bride would need balls of steel to hold her own.

At that point in Vitale's brooding reflections, Angel reappeared, looking abnormally subdued, and Vitale sprang upright with a question in his eyes.

'Your turn,' his older brother told him very drily without making any attempt to respond to Vitale's unspoken question for greater clarification.

Angel was visibly on edge, Vitale acknowledged in surprise, wondering what sensitive subject Charles Russell had broached with his eldest son. And then Vitale made a very good guess and he winced for his brother, because possibly their father had discovered that Angel had an illegitimate daughter he had yet to meet. That was Angel's biggest darkest secret, one he had shared only with Vitale, and it was likely to be an inflammatory topic for a man as family-orientated as their parent. It wasn't, however, a mistake that Vitale would ever make, Vitale thought with blazing confidence, because he never ever took risks in the birth-control department. He knew too well how narrow his options would be in that scenario if anything went wrong. Either he would have to face up to a colossal scandal or he would have to marry the woman concerned. Since the prospect of either option chilled him to the bone, he always played safe.

A still-handsome middle-aged man with greying hair, Charles Russell strode forward to give his taller son an enthusiastic hug. 'Sorry to have kept you waiting so long.'

'Not a problem,' Vitale said smoothly, refusing to admit that he had enraged his mother with his insistence on travelling to London rather than attending yet another court ceremonial function. Even so, his lean muscular length still stiffened in the circle of the older man's arms because while he was warmed by that open affection he was challenged to respond to it. Deep down somewhere inside him he was still the shrinking little boy whose mother had pushed him away with distaste at the age of two, telling him firmly that it was babyish and bad to still seek such attention.

'I need a favour and I thought you could deal with this thorny issue better than I could,' Charles admitted stiffly. 'Do you remember the house-keeper I employed at Chimneys?'

Vitale's eloquent dark eyes widened a little in disconcertion, lush black gold-tipped lashes framing his shrewd questioning gaze. He and Angel had spent countless school vacations at their father's country house on the Welsh border and Vitale had cherished every one of those holidays liberated from the stuffy traditions and formality of the Lerovian court. At Chimneys, an Elizabethan manor house, Vitale had been free as a bird, free to be a grubby little boy, a moody difficult adolescent, free to be whatever he wanted to be without the stress of constantly striving to meet arbitrary expectations.

'Not particularly. I don't really remember the staff.'

His father frowned, seemingly disappointed by that response. 'Her name was Peggy. She worked for me for years. She was married to the gardener, Robert Dickens.'

A sliver of recollection pierced Vitale's be-mused gaze, a bubble of memory about an old scandal finally rising to the surface. 'Red-haired woman, ran off with a toy boy,' he slotted in sardonically.

His tone made his father frown. 'Yes, that's the one. He was one of the trainee gardeners, shifty sort with a silver tongue,' he supplied. 'I always felt responsible for that mess.'

Vitale, who could not imagine getting involved or even being interested in an employee's private life, looked at the older man in frank astonishment. 'Why?'

'I saw bruises on Peggy on several occasions,' Charles admitted uncomfortably. 'I suspected Dickens of domestic abuse but I did nothing. I asked her several times if she was all right and she always assured me that she was. I should've done more.'

'I don't see what you could have done if she wasn't willing to make a complaint on her own behalf,' Vitale said dismissively, wondering where on earth this strange conversation could be leading while marvelling that his father could show visible distress when discussing the past life of a former servant. 'You weren't responsible.'

'Right and wrong isn't always that black and white,' Charles Russell replied grimly. 'If I'd been more supportive, more encouraging, possibly she might have given me her trust and told me the truth and I could have got her the help she and her daughter needed. Instead I was polite and distant and then she ran off with that smarmy little bastard.'

'I don't see what else you could have done. One should respect boundaries, particularly with staff,' Vitale declared, stiffening at the reference to Peggy's daughter but striving to conceal that reality. He had only the dimmest memory of Peggy Dickens but he remembered her daughter, Jazmine, well but probably only because Jazz figured in one of his own most embarrassing youthful recollections. He had little taste for looking back to the days before he had learned tact and discretion.

'No, you have to take a more human approach, Vitale. Staff are people too and sometimes they need help and understanding,' Charles argued.

Vitale didn't want to help or understand what motivated his staff at the bank or the palace; he simply wanted them to do their jobs to the best of their ability. He didn't get involved with employees on a personal level but, out of respect for his father, he resisted the urge to put his own point of view and instead tried to put the dialogue back on track. 'You said you needed a favour,' he reminded the older man.

Charles studied his son's lean, forbidding face in frustration, hating the fact that he recognised shades of his ex-wife's icy reserve and heartless detachment in Vitale. If there was one person Charles could be said to hate it would have to be the Queen of Lerovia, Sofia Castiglione. Yet he had loved her once, loved her to the edge of madness until he'd discovered that he was merely her dupe, her sperm donor for the heir she had needed for the Lerovian throne. Sofia's true love had been another woman, her closest friend, Cinzia, and from the moment Sofia had successfully conceived, Charles and their marriage as such had been very much surplus to requirements. But that was a secret the older man had promised to take to the grave with him. In the divorce settlement he had agreed to keep quiet in return for liberal access arrangements to his son and he had only ever regretted that silence afterwards when he had been forced to watch his ex-wife trying to suck the life out of Vitale with her constant carping and interference.

'Yes…the favour,' Charles recalled, forced back into the present. 'I've received a letter from Peggy's daughter, Jazmine, asking for my help. I want you to assess the situation and deal with it. I would do it myself but I'm going to be working abroad for the next few months and I don't have the time. I also thought you would handle it better because you knew each other well as children.'

Vitale's lean, strong, darkly good-looking face had tensed. In truth he had frozen where he stood at the threat of being forced to meet Jazz again. 'The situation?' he queried, playing for time.

The older man lifted a letter off the desk and passed it to him. 'The toy boy ripped Peggy off, forged her name on a stack of loans, plunged them into debt and *ruined* their financial standing!' he emphasised in ringing disgust. 'Now they're poor and struggling to survive. They've tried legal channels and got nowhere. Peggy's ill now and no longer able to work.'

Vitale's brow furrowed and he raised a silencing hand. 'But how is this trail of misfortune your business?' he asked without hesitation.

'Peggy Dickens has been on my conscience for years,' Charles confided grudgingly. 'I could have done something to help but I was too wary of causing offence so… I did nothing. All of this mess is on me and I don't want that poor woman suffering any more because I failed to act.'

'So, send her a cheque,' Vitale suggested, reeling from the display of guilt his father was revealing while he himself was struggling to see any connection or indeed any debt owed.

'Read the letter,' his father advised. 'Jazmine is asking for a job, somewhere to live and a loan, not a cheque. She's proud. She's not asking for a free handout but she's willing to do anything she can to help her mother.'

Vitale studied the envelope of what was obviously a begging letter with unconcealed distaste. More than ever he wanted to argue with his father's attitude. In Vitale's opinion, Charles owed his former employee and her daughter absolutely nothing. By the sound of it, Peggy Dickens had screwed up her life; however that was scarcely his father's fault.

'What do *you* want me to do?' Vitale asked finally, recognising that how he felt about the situation meant nothing in the face of his father's feelings.

Yet it amazed Vitale that his father could still be so incredibly emotional and sentimental and he often marvelled that two people as ridiculously dissimilar in character as his parents could ever have married.

'I want you to be compassionate and kind, *not* judgemental, *not* cynical, *not* cold,' Charles framed with anxious warning emphasis. 'And I know that will be a huge challenge for you but I also know that acknowledging that side of your nature will make you a better and stronger man in the process. Don't let your mother remake you in her image—never forget that you are *my* son too.'

Vitale almost flinched from the idea of being compassionate and kind. He didn't do stuff like that. He supported leading charities and always contributed to good causes but he had never done anything hands-on in that area, nor had he ever felt the need to do so. He was what he was: a bred-in-the-bone royal, cocooned from the real world by incredible privilege, an exclusive education and great wealth.

'I don't care what it costs to buy Peggy and her daughter out of trouble either,' his father added expansively. 'With you in charge of my investments, I can well afford the gesture. You don't need to save me money.'

'I'm a banker. Saving money and making a profit comes naturally,' Vitale said drily. 'And by the way, my mother is *not* remaking me in her image.'

Charles vented a roughened laugh. 'It may be graveyard humour but I wouldn't be a bit surprised if you find yourself engaged by the end of that ball next month! Sofia is a hell of a wheeler dealer. You should've refused to attend.'

'I may still do that. I'm no pushover,' his son stated coldly. 'So you want me to stage a rescue mission in your name?'

'With tact and generosity,' the older man added.

Exasperation leapt through Vitale, who used tact every day of his life because he could never be less than courteous in the face of the royal demands made of him. But no matter how onerous the demand Charles had made struck him, there was, nevertheless, a certain pride and satisfaction to the awareness that his father was *trusting* him to deal with a sensitive situation. He realised that he was also surprisingly eager to read Jazz's letter.

Jazz, a skinny-as-a-rail redhead, who had developed a massive crush on him when she was fourteen and he was eighteen. He had been wildly disconcerted that he rather than the friendlier, flirtier Angel had become the object of her admiration and he had screwed up badly, he acknowledged reluctantly, cracking a wounding joke about her that she had sadly overheard. But then Vitale had never been the sensitive sort and back then he had also essentially known very little about women because he had stayed a virgin for many years longer than Angel. But, not surprisingly, Jazz had hated him after that episode and in many ways it had been a relief to no longer be the centre of her attention and the awful tongue-tied silences that had afflicted her in his presence. In the space of one awkward summer, the three of them had travelled from casual pseudo friendship to stroppy, strained discomfiture and then she and her mother had mercifully disappeared out of their lives.

Compassionate... Kind, Vitale reminded himself as he stood outside his father's office reading Jazz's letter, automatically rating it for use of English, spelling and conciseness. Of course it

had been written on the computer because Jazz
was severely dyslexic. Dyslexic and clumsy, he
recalled helplessly, always tripping and bump-
ing into things. The letter told a tale of woe that
could have featured as a Greek tragedy and his
sculpted mouth tightened, his momentary amusement dying away. She wanted help for her mother
but only on her own terms. She wanted a job but
only had experience of working as a checkout
operator and a cleaner.

Per carita…for pity's sake, what did she think
his father was going to find for her to do on the
back of such slender talents? Even so, the letter
was pure Jazz, feisty and gauche and crackling
with brick-wall obstinacy. An ordinary woman,
he thought abstractedly, an ordinary woman
with extraordinarily beautiful green eyes. Her
eyes wouldn't have changed, he reasoned. And
you couldn't get more ordinary than Jazz, who
thought a soup spoon or a fish fork or a nap-
kin was pure unnecessary aristocratic affecta-
tion. And she *was*, evidently, badly in need of
money…

A faint smile tilted Vitale's often grim mouth. He didn't need a stunning beauty to act as his partner at the palace ball and he was quite sure that if he hired the right experts Jazz could be transformed into something reasonably presentable. Having a partner for the ball to fend off other women would make sense, he acknowledged reluctantly. But shooting Zac down in flames would undeniably be the most satisfying aspect of the whole affair. Jazz might be ordinary and dyslexic but she was also clever and a quick study.

Vitale strolled back to his younger brother's side with a rare smile on his wide sensual mouth. 'You're up next but before you go…the bet,' he specified in an undertone. 'Remember that blonde waitress who wanted nothing to do with you last week and accused you of harassment?'

Zac frowned, disconcerted colour highlighting his high cheekbones at that reminder of his rare failure to impress a woman.

'Bring her to the ball acting all lovelorn and clingy and suitably polished up and you have a deal on the bet,' Vitale completed, throwing down the gauntlet of challenge with pleasure while recalling the very real hatred he had seen in that woman's eyes. For once, Zac, the smooth-talking seducer, would have his work cut out for him…

Jazz straightened her aching back at the check-out because she had worked a very long day. Her schedule had kicked off at dawn with a cleaning shift at a nearby hotel and then she had got a call to step in for a sick workmate at the till in the supermarket where she earned extra cash on a casual basis. Both her jobs were casual, poorly paid and unreliable. But some work was better than no work, she reminded herself doggedly, better than living on welfare, which would have distressed her mother more even though that choice would have left mother and daughter somewhat better off.

But while Peggy Dickens had raised her daughter to be a worker rather than a whinger or a free-loader, Jazz still occasionally let her thoughts drift into a dream world where she had got to complete the education that would have equipped her with a degree that enabled her to chase better-paid jobs and climb an actual career ladder. Unfortunately, the chaos of her private life had prevented her from, what was that phrase... achieving her full potential? Her full pink mouth curled at the corners with easy amusement for who was to say that she was worth any more than the work she was currently doing? No point getting too big for her boots and imagining she might have been more, not when she came from such humble roots.

Her mother had been a housekeeper, who married a gardener and lived in accommodation provided by their employer. Nobody in Jazz's family tree had ever owned a house or earned a university degree and Peggy had been bemused when her daughter had chosen to continue her education and aim so much higher than any of her ancestors, but her mother had been proud as well.

And then their lives had gone down the tubes again and Jazz had had to put practicality first yet again. Unfortunately, it was virtually impossible to regain lost ground. Jazz had almost had a nervous breakdown studying to overcome the drawbacks of changing schools three times over during her teen years. She had not wept when her parents' unhappy marriage had finally broken down because her father had often beaten up her mother and had hurt Jazz as well when she had been foolish enough to try and intervene. She had grieved, though, when her father had died unexpectedly only a couple of years afterwards without having once tried to see her again. Evidently her father had never much cared for his only child and that knowledge had hurt. She had been sincerely aghast, however, when her mother, Peggy fell in love with Jeff Starling, a much younger man.

Love could be the biggest risk out there for a woman, Jazz reflected with an inner shiver of repulsion, most especially the kind of love that could persuade an otherwise sensible woman into jumping straight out of the frying pan into the fire.

But there were other kinds of love as well, she reminded herself comfortingly, life-enriching family connections that soothed and warmed, no matter how bad life got. When Jeff's bad debts had ensured that Peggy and her daughter couldn't even get a lease on a rental property, Peggy's kid sister, Clodagh, had given them a home in her tiny apartment. When Peggy had been diagnosed with breast cancer, Clodagh had stepped back from her little jewellery business to shepherd her sister to her appointments and treatments and nurse her tenderly while Jazz tried to keep on earning what little money she could.

Bolstered by those more positive thoughts, Jazz finished her shift and walked home in the dusk. Her phone pinged and she dug it out, green eyes widening when she read the text with difficulty. It was short and sweet, beginning, *re: letter to Charles Russell.*

Holy Moses, she thought in shock, Charles Russell was actually willing to meet her to discuss her mother's plight! Ten o'clock tomorrow morning, not much notice, she conceded ruefully, but beggars couldn't be choosers, could they be?

In desperation, she had written to her mother's former employer pleading for help. Charles was a kind man and generous to a fault but almost ten years down the road from Peggy's employment, Jazz had not even expected to receive a reply. That letter had been a long shot, the product of a particularly sleepless night when she was stressing about how she could best help her mother with the stable, stress-free existence she needed to recover from what had proved to be a gruelling treatment schedule. After all, they couldn't live with Clodagh for ever. Clodagh had sacrificed a lot to take them in off the street, not least a boyfriend, who had vanished once the realities of Clodagh's new caring role had sunk in. Ironically, Jazz had not thought that there was the remotest possibility that her letter to Charles Russell would even be acknowledged...

A hot feeling of shame crept up inside her, burning her pale porcelain skin with mortified heat because the instant she had posted that letter, she had squirmed with regret over the sacrifice of her pride. Hadn't she been raised to stand on her own feet? Yet sometimes, no matter what you did and no matter how hard you worked, you needed a helping hand to climb up out of a ditch. And evidently, Charles Russell had taken pity on their plight and maybe, just maybe, he had recognised that he could offer his assistance in some way. With somewhere to live? With employment? Hope sprang high, dousing the shame of having written and posted a begging letter. Any help, no matter how small or seemingly insignificant, would be welcome, she told herself sternly.

Stuffing her phone back in her pocket, Jazz unlocked the door of the apartment, suppressing a sigh when she saw the mess in the living and kitchen area. Clodagh wasn't tidy and she wasn't much for cleaning or doing dishes or laundry but Jazz did what she could to pick up the slack, always conscious that she lived in Clodagh's home while remaining equally aware that her neat freak of a mother found it depressing to live in such messy surroundings. But there wasn't much that could be done to make a one-bedroom apartment stretch to the occupation of three adults, one of whom was still struggling to regain her strength. The treatments might have concluded but Peggy was still in the recovery phase. Clodagh shared the bedroom with her sister but when Peggy had a restless night, Clodagh took the couch and Jazz slept in a sleeping bag on the floor.

'I had a good day,' Peggy announced chirpily from in front of the television, a thin-faced, pale and still-frail-looking woman in her forties. 'I went for a walk in the park after mass.'

'That's brilliant,' Jazz said, bending down to kiss the older woman's cheek, the baby fine fuzz of her mother's regrown hair brushing her brow and bringing tears to her tired eyes. The hair had grown again in white, rather then red, and Peggy had refused to consider dying it as Clodagh had suggested, confessing that as far as she was concerned any hair was better than no hair.

Jazz was intensely relieved that her mother was regaining her energy and had an excellent prognosis. Having initially faced the terrifying prospect that she might lose her mother, she was merely grateful to still have her and was keen to improve the older woman's life as much as possible.

'Hungry?' Jazz prompted.

'Not really,' Peggy confessed guiltily.

'I'll make a lovely salad and you can do your best with it,' Jazz declared, knowing it was imperative to encourage her mother to regain some of the weight she had lost.

'Clodagh's visiting her friend, Rose,' Peggy told her. 'She asked me to join them but I was too tired and I like to see you when you come in from work.'

Suppressing her exhaustion, Jazz began to clean up the kitchen, neatly stowing away her aunt's jewellery-making supplies in their designated clear boxes and then embarking on the dishes before preparing the salad that was presently the only option that awakened her mother's appetite. While she worked, she chattered, sharing a little gossip about co-workers, bringing her working day home with her to brighten her mother's more restricted lifestyle and enjoy the sound of her occasional chuckle.

They sat down at the table to eat. Jazz was mentally running through her tiny wardrobe to select a suitable outfit for her morning appointment with Charles Russell. Giving up the luxury of their own home had entailed selling off almost all their belongings because there had been no money to spare to rent a storage facility and little room for anything extra in Clodagh's home. Jazz had a worn black pencil skirt and jeans and shorts and a few tops and that was literally all. She had learned to be grateful for the uniform she wore at both her jobs because it meant that she could get by with very few garments. Formality insisted on her wearing the skirt, she conceded ruefully, and her only pair of high heels.

She had not mentioned her letter to either her mother or her aunt because she hadn't expected anything to come of it and, in the same way, she could not quite accept that she had been given an appointment. Indeed, several times before she finally dropped off to sleep on the couch that evening, she had to dig out her phone and anxiously reread that text to persuade herself that it wasn't a figment of her imagination.

Early the next morning, fearful of arriving late, Jazz crossed London by public transport and finally arrived outside a tall town house. She had been surprised not to be invited to the older man's office where she had sent the letter, but perhaps he preferred a less formal and more discreet setting for their meeting. She was even more surprised by the size and exclusive location of the house. Charles Russell had once been married to a reigning queen, she reminded herself wryly. A queen who, on her only fleeting visit to her former husband's country home, had treated Jazz's mother like the dirt beneath her expensively shod feet.

But Charles had been infinitely kinder and more gracious with his staff, she recalled fondly, remembering the older man's warm smiles and easy conversation with her even though she was only his housekeeper's daughter. Unlike his royal ex-wife and second son, he was not a snob and had never rated people in importance solely according to their social or financial status. A *kind* man, she repeated doggedly to herself to quell her leaping nervous tension as she rang the doorbell.

A woman who spoke little English, and what she did speak was with an impenetrable accent, ushered her into an imposing hall furnished with gleaming antiques and mirrors. Scanning her intimidating surroundings and feeling very much like an interloper, Jazz began to revise up her estimate of Charles Russell's wealth.

Another door was cast open into what looked like a home office and a man sprang up from behind the solid wooden desk.

Jazz was so aghast by the recognition that roared through her slender frame that she froze on the threshold of the room and stared in dismay, all her natural buoyance draining away as though someone very cruel had stabbed a pin into her tender flesh and deflated her like a balloon. It was Vitale, not his father, and that had to be... Her. Worst. Nightmare. *Ever...*

CHAPTER TWO

VITALE STARED, TAKEN aback by the woman in the doorway because she was a knockout, the kind of vibrant beauty who turned male heads in the street with her streaming red-gold curls and slender, supple body. About the only things that hadn't changed about Jazz were her eyes, green as jade set in a triangular face, skin as translucent as the finest pale porcelain and a surprisingly full pink mouth, little white teeth currently plucking at her lower lip as she gazed at him in almost comical horror.

'Come in and close the door,' Vitale urged smoothly, wondering how on earth he was going to teach her to stop wearing her every thought on her face while also wondering why he found that candidness attractive.

Jazz made a valiant attempt to stage a recovery

even though every ounce of her hard-won confidence had been blown out of the water. Shock waves were travelling through her slight body. One glimpse of Vitale and her brain was mush at best and at worst sending her back in time to a very vulnerable period she did not want to remember. But there Vitale was, as sleek and drop-dead gorgeous as he had ever been and so compelling in his undeniable masculine beauty that it took terrible effort to even look away from him.

What was it about Vitale, what crazy weakness in her made him seem so appealing? His brother, Angel Valtinos, had been too pretty and vain to draw her and she had never once looked at Angel in *that* way. But then, Vitale was a much more complex and fascinating creature, all simmering, smouldering intensity and conflicts below the smooth, sophisticated surface he wore for the world. Those perfect manners and that cool reserve of his couldn't mask the intense emotion he held in restraint behind those stunning dark golden eyes. And he was *so* sexy. Every sinuous movement of his lean, muscular body, every downward dip of his gold-tipped, outrageously thick black lashes, and every quirk of his beautifully shaped sensual mouth contributed to his ferocious sex appeal. It was little wonder that when she had finally been of an age to crush on a man, her attention had immediately locked onto Vitale, even though Vitale had found it quite impossible to treat her like a friend.

Jazz closed the door in a harried movement and walked towards the chair set in front of the desk. You're a grown-up now. The embarrassing stuff you did as a kid no longer matters, her defences were instructing her at a frantic pitch, and so intent was she on listening to that face-saving voice that she didn't notice the edge of the rug in front of her. Her spiky heel caught on the fringe and she pitched forward with a startled cry.

And Vitale was there at supersonic speed, catching her before she could fall and steadying her with a strong arm to her spine. The heat of his hand at her waist startled her almost as much as his sudden proximity. She jerked skittishly away from him to settle down heavily into the chair but her nostrils flared appreciatively. The dark sensual scent of his spicy cologne overlying warm earthy male plunged her senses into overdrive.

Vitale had finally touched her, Vitale, who avoided human contact as much as possible, she recalled abstractedly, striving not to look directly at him until she had got her stupid brain back on line. He would be smiling: she *knew* that. Her clumsiness had always amused him because he was as lithe and sure-footed as a cat. Now he unnerved her more by not returning to the other side of the desk and instead lounging back against it with unusual casualness, staying far too close for comfort, a long, muscular, powerful thigh within view that did nothing to restore her composure.

Her fingertips dug into her palms as she fought for calm. 'I was expecting to meet with your father,' she admitted thinly.

'Charles asked me to handle this,' Vitale confided, barely resisting the urge to touch the wild corkscrew mane of flaming ringlets tumbling across her shoulders with gleaming electric vigour. So, he liked the hair and the eyes, he reasoned, wondering why he had abandoned his usual formality to sit so close to her, wondering why the simple smell of soap that she emanated was so surpassingly sexy, wondering why that slender body with its delicate curves, tiny waist and shapely legs should suddenly seem so very tempting a package. Because she wasn't his type, not even remotely his type, he told himself sternly. He had always gone for tall, curvy blondes, redheads being too bright and brash for his tastes.

On the other hand he had never wanted so badly to touch a woman's hair and that weird prompting unnerved him into springing upright again and striding across the room. The dulled throb of awakening desire at his groin inspired him with another stab of incredulity because since adulthood he had always been fully in control of that particular bodily affliction.

'I can't think why,' Jazz said, dry-mouthed, unbearably conscious of him looming over her for that split second before he moved away because he stood well over six feet tall and she barely made a couple of inches over five foot.

'I assure you that the exchange will work out very much to your advantage,' Vitale husked, deciding that his uncharacteristic interest had simply been stimulated by the challenge that he now saw lay ahead of him: the transformation of Jazz. Number one on the agenda would be persuading her to stop biting her nails. Number two would be ditching the giant fake gold hoop earrings. Number three would be avoiding any shoe that looked as if a stripper might wear it.

Jazz let slip a very rude startled word in response to that unlikely statement.

And number four would be cleaning up her vocabulary, Vitale reflected, glad to so clearly see her flaws so that he could concentrate on the practicalities of his challenge, rather than dwell on any aspect that could be deemed personal.

'Don't swear,' Vitale told her.

Jazz reddened as high as her hairline because she could remember him saying the same thing to her when she was about twelve years old while warning her that once she became accustomed to using such words, using them would become an embarrassing habit. And being Vitale, he had been infuriatingly bang on target with that advice. Using curse words had made her seem a little cooler at school back then…well, as cool as you could be with bright red hair and a flat chest, puberty having passed her by for far longer than she cared to recall, making her an anomaly amongst her peers.

'You need financial help,' Vitale pointed out with undiplomatic bluntness, keen to get right to the heart of the matter and remind her of her situation. If he neglected to remind her of her boundaries, Jazz would be a stubborn, defiant baggage and hard to handle.

Living up to that assessment, Jazz flew upright, earrings swinging wildly in the torrent of her burnished hair, colour marking her cheekbones, highlighting eyes bright with angry defensiveness. 'I did *not* ask for money from your father!' she snapped back at him.

'Employment, a home, the settlement of outstanding loans?' Vitale reminded her with cruel precision. 'How could any of those aspirations be achieved without someone laying out a considerable amount of money on your behalf?'

The angry colour drained from her disconcerted face, perspiration breaking out on her short upper lip as he threw her crash-bang up against hard reality, refusing to allow her to deny the obvious. She stared back at him, trapped like a rabbit in headlights and hating him for it. Mortification claimed her along with a healthy dose of shame that she should have put herself in such a position and with Vitale of all people. Vitale, who had never treated her like an equal as Angel had done, Vitale who had never for one moment forgotten that she was essentially a servant's child, thrown into the brothers' company only by proximity.

Vitale watched Jazz crash down from fury to bitter, embarrassed acceptance. *Sì*…yes, he told himself with satisfaction, that had been the right note to sound. She dropped back into the chair, sunset heat warming her cheeks and bowing her head on her slender neck.

'And the good news is that I'm willing to provide that money *if*...in return, you are willing to do something for me.'

'I can't imagine anything that I could do for you,' Jazz told him truthfully.

'Then listen and learn,' Vitale advised, poised by the window with the light glimmering over his luxuriant blue-black hair, the suave olive planes of his cheekbones taut. 'At the end of next month my mother is throwing a ball at the palace. Her objective is to match me up with a future bride and the guest list will be awash with young women who have what the Queen deems to be the right pedigree and background.'

Jazz was staring at him now in wide-eyed wonderment. 'Are you kidding me?'

His sculpted mouth quirked. 'I wish I was.'

Her smooth brow furrowed as she collided with hot dark golden eyes and suddenly found it fatally difficult to breathe. 'You're angry about it.'

'*Oviamente*...of course I am. I'm nowhere near

the stage in life where I want to get married and settle down. But having considered the situation, it has occurred to me,' Vitale murmured quietly, 'that arriving at the ball with what appears to be a partner, whom I'm seriously involved with, would be my best defence. I want you to be that partner.'

'Me?' Jazz gaped at him in disbelief, green eyes a pool of verdant jade bemusement as she gazed up at him, soft full pink lips slightly parted. 'How could *I* be your partner? I couldn't go to a royal ball!'

'Suitably gowned and refined, you could,' Vitale disagreed, choosing his words with care because the throb below his belt went up tempo when he focused on that soft, oh, so inviting full lower lip of hers. 'But you would have to be willing to work at the presentation required because you would have to both *look* like and *act* like the sort of woman I would bring to a royal ball.'

'Impossible,' Jazz told him. 'It would take more than a fancy dress and not swearing.'

'It would but, given that we have several weeks

at our disposal in which to prepare, I think you could easily do it,' Vitale declared, shocking her even more with that vote of apparent confidence. 'And whether you successfully contrive the pretence or fail it, I will still pay you well for trying to make the grade.'

'But why me?' Jazz spluttered in a rush. 'Why someone like me? Surely you have a friend who could pretend to be something more for the evening?'

'Why you? Because someone bet me that I couldn't pass off an ordinary woman as a socialite at a royal ball,' Vitale delivered, opting for the truth. 'You fit the bill and I prefer to *pay* for the pretence rather than ask anyone to do me a favour. In addition, as it will be in your best interests to succeed, you will make more effort to meet the standard required.'

Jazz was transfixed by his admission. 'A bet,' she echoed weakly. 'To go to all that effort and put out money simply to win a bet…it would be absurd.'

Vitale shrugged a wide shoulder, sheathed in

the finest silk and wool blend, the jacket of his exquisitely well-tailored suit sliding open to reveal his torso, lean, strong muscles flexing below the thin cotton shirt. Her mouth ran dry because he was a work of art on a physical level, every silken, honed line of his lean, powerful physique hard and muscular and fit. 'Does the absurdity of it have to concern you?'

'I guess not...' she said uncertainly, knowing that what was what he wanted her to say, playing it sensibly by ear and reluctant to argue while momentarily lost in the dark, exciting challenge of his hard, assessing gaze.

She had almost forgotten what that excitement felt like, had never felt it since in a man's radius and had been much too young and naïve to feel its mortifying bite at the age of fourteen. She had experienced what felt like all the sensations of a grown woman while still trapped in the body of an undeveloped child. Unsurprisingly, struggling to deal with that adolescent flood of sexual awakening had made her so silent, so awkward and so wretched around Vitale that she had been filled with self-loathing and shame.

Now that same excitement was curling up hot in the pit of her stomach and spreading dangerous tendrils of awareness to more sensitive places. She felt her nipples pinch tight below her tee shirt and her small breasts swell with the shaken breath she snatched in as she willed the torture to stop. But her body's reaction to Vitale had never been something she could control and the inexorable pulse of that heat between her thighs made her feel murderously uncomfortable and foolish.

A bet, she was still thinking with even greater incredulity, desperate to stop thinking about her physical reaction to him. Vitale was willing to invest good money in an attempt to win a bet. That was beyond her capacity to imagine and she thought it was very wrong. In her experience money was precious and should be reserved to cover the necessities of life: rent, heat and food. She had never lived in a world where money was easily obtained or where there was ever enough of it. Even when her parents had still been together, having sufficient money simply to live had been a constant source of concern, thanks to her father's addiction to online betting.

But Vitale lived at a very different level, she reminded herself ruefully. He took money for granted, had never gone without and could probably never understand how bone-deep appalled she was by his light-hearted attitude and how even more hostile she was to any form of gambling.

'I don't approve of gambling,' she admitted tightly, thinking of the families destroyed by the debts accrued and the addicts who could not break free of their dream of a big win.

'It's *not*—'

'It *is* gambling,' Jazz cut in with assurance. 'You're betting on the outcome of something that can't be predicted and you may make a loss.'

'That's my problem, not yours,' Vitale delivered without hesitation. 'You need to think about how this arrangement would benefit you. I would settle those loans and find a place of your choosing for you and your mother to live. I don't know what I could offer on the employment front but I'm sure I could provide some help. The decision is yours. I'll give you twenty-four hours to think it over.'

Her green eyes flared in anger again. 'You haven't even told me what would be involved if I accepted!'

'Obviously you'd have to have a makeover and a certain amount of coaching before you could meet the demands of the role,' Vitale imparted, marvelling that she hadn't eagerly snatched at his offer straight away. 'Right now you're drowning in debt and you have no options. I can *give* you options.'

It was the bald truth and she hated him for spelling it out. If wishes were horses, then beggars would ride, she chanted inside her head. Being badly in debt meant that she and her mother had virtually no choices and little chance of improving their lot in life. She swallowed hard on that humiliating reality that put Vitale squarely in the driver's seat. A makeover, *coaching*? Inwardly she cringed but it was no surprise to her that she would not do as she was. She would never be good enough for Vitale on any level. She didn't have the right breeding or background and found it hard to credit that even a makeover would raise her to the standard required by a highly sophisticated royal prince, who couldn't even drink beer out of a bottle without looking uncomfortable.

'Yes, if I can trust you, you could give us options,' she conceded flatly. 'But how do I know that you will keep your promises if this doesn't work?'

Vitale stiffened as though she had slapped him. 'I give you my word,' he bit out witheringly. 'Surely that should be sufficient?'

'There are very few people in this world that I trust,' Jazz admitted apologetically.

'I will have a legal agreement drawn up, then,' Vitale breathed with icy cool. 'Will that satisfy you?'

Jazz lifted her head high, barely able to credit that she was bargaining with Vitale. 'We don't need a legal agreement for something this crazy. You get rid of the loans first as a show of faith,' she dared. 'I'm fed up trying to protect my mother from debt collectors.'

'I don't understand why you're even trying to repay loans that were fraudulently taken out in your mother's name.'

'It's incredibly difficult to prove that it *was* fraud. Jeff died in an accident last year and he wasn't prosecuted. A solicitor tried to sort it out for Mum but we didn't have enough proof to clear her name and she won't declare herself bankrupt because she sees that as the ultimate humiliation,' she explained, wanting him to know that they had explored every possible avenue. 'She was ill and going through chemo at the time and I didn't want to put any more pressure on her.'

'You give me all the paperwork for the loans and I will have them dealt with,' Vitale asserted. 'But if I do so, I will own you body and soul until the end of next month.'

'Nobody will *ever* own me body and soul.'

'Apart from me for the next couple of months,' Vitale contradicted with lethal cool. 'If I pay up-front, I call the shots and you do as you're told, whether you like it or not.'

Jazz blinked in bewilderment, wondering how she had got herself into the situation she was in. He thought he had her agreement and why wouldn't he when she had bargained the terms with him? Even the prospect of those dreadful loans being settled knocked her for six. A visit or a phone call from a debt collector upset her mother for days afterwards, depriving her of the peace of mind she needed to rebuild her life and her health. How could Jazz possibly turn her back on an offer like Vitale's? Nobody else was going to give them the opportunity to make a fresh start.

'You haven't given me a chance to think this through,' she argued shakily.

'You were keen enough to set out your conditions,' Vitale reminded her drily.

And her face flamed because she was in no position to protest that assumption. The offer of money had cut right through her fine principles and her aversion to gambling. The very idea that she could sort out her mother's problems and give her a happier and more secure future had thoroughly seduced her.

'You'll move in here as soon as possible,' Vitale decreed.

Her head flew up, corkscrew curls tumbling across her shoulders, green eyes huge. 'Move in here? With *you*?'

'How else can we achieve this? You must be readily available. How else can I supervise? And if I take you to the ball it will be assumed we are lovers, and should anyone do a check, it will be clear that you were already living here in my house,' Vitale pointed out. 'If we are to succeed, you have to consider little supporting details of that nature.'

Jazz studied him, aghast. 'I can't move in with you!' she gasped. 'What am I supposed to tell my mother?'

Vitale shrugged with magnificent lack of interest. 'Whatever suits. That I've given you a job? That we're having an affair? I don't care.'

Her feathery lashes fluttered rapidly, her animated face troubled as she pondered that problem. 'Yes, I could admit I sent the letter to your father and say I've been offered a live-in job and my aunt would look after Mum, so I wouldn't need to worry about her,' she reasoned out loud. 'Would I still be able to work? I have two part-time jobs.'

'No. You won't have the time. I'll pay you a salary for the duration of your stay here,' Vitale added, reading her expression to register the dismay etched there at the news that she would not be able to continue in paid employment.

'This is beginning to sound like a very expensive undertaking for you,' Jazz remarked uncomfortably, her face more flushed than ever.

'My choice,' Vitale parried dismissively while he wondered how far that flush extended beneath her clothing and whether that scattering of freckles across the bridge of her nose was repeated anywhere else on her delicate body. He wondered dimly why such an imperfection should seem even marginally appealing and why he should suddenly be picturing her naked with all the eagerness of a sex-starved teenage boy. He tensed, thoroughly unsettled by his complete loss of concentration and detachment.

'I'll say you've offered me a job,' Jazz said abruptly, her thoughts leaping ahead of her. 'Are there many art works in this house?'

Vitale frowned and stared enquiringly at her. 'Yes, but—'

'Then I could say that I was cataloguing them or researching them for you,' Jazz announced with satisfaction. 'I was only six months off completing a BA in History of Art when Mum's life fell apart and I had to drop out. I may not have attained my degree but I have done placements in museums and galleries, so I do have good working experience.'

'If what you're telling me is true, why are you working in a shop and as a cleaner?'

'Because without that degree certificate, I can't work in my field. I'll finish my studies once life has settled down again,' she said with wry acceptance.

Vitale struggled to imagine the added stress of

studying at degree level in spite of her dyslexia and all its attendant difficulties and a grudging respect flared in him because she had fought her disability and refused to allow it to hold her back. 'Why did you drop out?'

'Mum's second husband, Jeff, died suddenly and she was inconsolable.' Jazz grimaced. 'That was long before the debt collectors began calling and we found out about the loans Jeff had taken out and forged her name on. I took time out from university but things went downhill very quickly from that point and I couldn't leave Mum alone. We were officially homeless and living in a boarding house when she was diagnosed with cancer and that was when my aunt asked us to move in with her. It's been a rough couple of years.'

Vitale made no comment, backing away from the personal aspects of the information she was giving him, deeming them not his business, not his concern. He needed to concentrate on the end game alone and that was preparing her for the night of the ball.

'How soon can you move in?' he prompted impatiently.

Jazz stiffened at that blunt question. 'This week sometime?' she suggested.

'I'll send a car to collect you tomorrow at nine and pack for a long stay. We don't have time to waste,' Vitale pronounced as she slid out of the seat and straightened, the pert swell of her small breasts prominent in a tee shirt that was a little too tight, the skirt clinging to her slim thighs and the curve of her bottom, the fabric shiny with age. Her ankles looked ridiculously narrow and delicate above those clodhopper sandals with their towering heels. The pulse at his groin that nagged at his usually well-disciplined body went crazy.

'Tomorrow's a little soon, surely?' Jazz queried in dismay.

Vitale compressed his lips, exasperated by his physical reaction to her. 'We have a great deal to accomplish.'

'Am I really that unpresentable?' Jazz heard herself ask sharply.

'Cinderella *shall* go to the ball,' Vitale retorted with diplomatic conviction, ducking an answer that was obvious to him even if it was not to her. 'When I put my mind to anything, I make it work.'

In something of a daze, Jazz refused the offer of a car to take her home and muttered the fiction that she had some shopping to do. In truth she only ever shopped at the supermarket, not having the money to spare for treats. But she knew she needed time to get her head clear and work out what she was going to say before she went home again, and that was how she ended up sitting in a park in the spring sunshine, feeling much as though she had had a run-in with a truck that had squashed her flat.

'She's as flat as an ironing board, not to mention the hideous rag-doll hair but, worst of all, she's a *child*, Angel...'

Vitale's well-bred voice filtered down through the years to sound afresh inside her head. Angel spoke Greek and Vitale spoke Italian, so the brothers had always communicated in English.

Angel had been teasing Vitale about her crush and of course Jazz had been so innocent at fourteen that it had not even occurred to her that the boys had noticed her infatuation, and that unwelcome discovery as much as Vitale's withering description of her lack of attractiveness had savaged Jazz. She had known she wasn't much to look at, but knowing and having it said out loud by the object of her misplaced affections had cut her deep. Furthermore, being deemed to be still a child, even though in hindsight she now agreed with that conviction, had hurt even more at the time and she had hated him for it. She still remembered the dreadful moment when the boys had appeared out of the summerhouse and had seen her standing there, white as a sheet on the path, realising that they had been overheard.

Angel had grimaced but Vitale had looked genuinely appalled. At eighteen, Vitale hadn't had the ability to hide his feelings that he did as an adult, and at that moment Vitale had recognised how upset she was and had deeply regretted his words, his troubled dark golden eyes telegraphing that truth. Not that he would have admitted it or said anything, though, or even apologised, she conceded wryly, because royalty did not admit fault or indeed do anything that lowered the dignified cool front of polished perfection.

"Cinderella shall go to the ball," he had said as if he were conferring some enormous honour on her. As if she cared about his stupid fancy ball, or his even more stupid bet! But she *did* care about her mother, she reminded herself ruefully, and if Vitale was willing to help her family, she was willing to eat dirt, strain every sinew to please and play Cinderella…even if the process did sting her pride and humiliate her and there would be no glass slipper waiting for her!

CHAPTER THREE

'I'M ONLY WORRIED because you had such a thing for him when you were young.' Peggy Starling rested anxious green eyes on her daughter's pink cheeks. 'Living in the same house with him now, working for him.'

'He's a prince, Mum,' Jazz pointed out, wishing her colour didn't change so revealingly, wishing she could honestly swear that she now found Vitale totally unattractive. 'I'm not an idiot.'

'But you were never really aware of him being a royal at Chimneys because Mr Russell wanted him treated like any other boy while he was staying there and his title was never used,' her mother reasoned uncomfortably. 'I just don't want you getting hurt again.'

'Oh, for goodness' sake, Peggy, stop fussing!' Clodagh interrupted impatiently, a small woman in her late thirties with the trademark family red hair cut short. 'Jazz is a grown woman now and she's been offered a decent job and a nice place to live for a couple of months. Don't spoil it for her!'

Jazz gave her aunt a grateful glance. 'The extra money will come in useful and I'll visit regularly,' she promised.

Her possessions in a bag, Jazz hugged her mother and her aunt and took her leave, walking downstairs, because the lift was always broken, and out to the shabby street where a completely out-of-place long black shiny limousine awaited her. Amusement filtered through her nerves when she saw that the muscular driver was out patrolling round the car, keen to protect his pride and joy from a hovering cluster of jeering kids.

Vitale strode out of his office when he heard the slam of the front door of the town house because somewhere in the back of his mind he couldn't quite credit that he was doing what he was doing and that Jazz would actually turn up. More fool him, he thought sardonically, reckoning that the financial help he was offering would be more than sufficient as a bait on the hook of her commitment.

He scanned her slim silhouette in jeans and a sweater, wondering if he ought to be planning to take before and after photos for some silly scrapbook while acknowledging that her hair, her skin, her eyes, her truly perfect little face required no improvement whatsoever. His attention fell in surprise to the bulging carrier bag she carried.

'I told you to pack for a long stay,' he reminded her with a frown. 'I meant bring everything you require to be comfortable.'

Jazz shrugged. 'This *is* everything I own,' she said tightly.

'It can't be,' Vitale pronounced in disbelief, accustomed to women who travelled with suitcases that ran into double figures.

'Being homeless strips you of your possessions pretty efficiently,' Jazz told him drily. 'I only kept *one* snow globe, my first one…'

And a faint shard of memory pierced Vitale's brain. He recalled her dragging him and Angel into her bedroom to show off her snow globe collection when they must all have been very young. She had had three of those ugly plastic domes and the first one had had an evil little Santa Claus figure inside it. He and Angel had surveyed the girlie display, unimpressed. 'They're beautiful,' Vitale had finally squeezed out, trying to be kind under the onslaught of her expectant green eyes, and knowing that a lie was necessary because she was tiny, and he still remembered the huge smile she had given him, which had assured him that he had said the right thing.

'The Santa one?' he queried.

Disconcerted, Jazz stared back at him in astonishment. 'You remember that?'

'It stayed with me. I've never seen a snow globe since,' Vitale told her truthfully, relieved to be off the difficult subject of her having been homeless at one stage, while censuring himself for not having registered the practical consequences of such an upsetting experience.

'So, when do the lessons start?' Jazz prompted.

'Come into my office. The housekeeper will show you to your room later.'

Jazz straightened her slender spine and tried hard not to stare at Vitale, which was an enormous challenge when he looked so striking in an exquisitely tailored dark grey suit that outlined his lean, powerful physique to perfection, a white shirt and dark silk tie crisp at his brown throat. So, he's gorgeous, *get over it*, she railed inwardly at herself until the full onslaught of spectacular dark golden eyes heavily fringed by black lashes drove even that sensible thought from her mind.

'First you get measured up for a new wardrobe. Next you get elocution.'

'Elocution?' Jazz gasped.

For all the world as though he had suggested keelhauling her under Angel's yacht, Vitale thought helplessly.

'You can't do this with a noticeable regional accent,' Vitale sliced in. 'Stop reacting to everything I say as though it's personal.'

'It *is* freaking personal when someone says you don't talk properly!' Jazz slashed back at him furiously, her colour heightened.

'And the language,' Vitale reminded her without skipping a beat, refusing to be sidetracked from his ultimate goal. 'I'm not insulting you. Stop personalising this arrangement. You are being prepared for an acting role.'

The reminder was a timely one, but it still struck Jazz as very personal when a man looked at her and decided he had to change virtually everything about her. She compressed her lips and said instead, '*Freaking* is not a bad word.'

Vitale released a groan, gold-tipped lashes flying high while he noticed the fullness of her soft pink lips even when she was trying to fold them flat, and his body succumbed to an involuntary stirring he fiercely resented. 'Are you going to argue about everything?'

Common sense assailed Jazz and she bent down to rummage industriously in her carrier bag. 'Not if you settle these loans,' she muttered in as apologetic a tone as she could manage while still hating him for picking out her every flaw.

Vitale watched her settle a small heap of crumpled papers on his desk while striving to halter her temper, a battle he could read on her eloquent face. He supposed he could live with 'freaking' if he had to. For that matter he knew several socialites who swore like troopers and he wondered if he was setting his expectations rather too high, well aware that if he had a flaw, and he wasn't willing to acknowledge that he *did*, it was a desire for perfection.

'After elocution comes lessons in etiquette,' he informed her doggedly, suppressing that rare instant of self-doubt. 'You have to know how to address the other guests, many of whom will have titles.'

'It sounds like a *really* fun-packed morning,' Jazz pronounced acidly.

Amusement flashed through Vitale but he crushed it at source, reluctant to encourage her irreverence. Of course, he wasn't used to any woman behaving around him the way Jazz did. Jazz had smoothly shifted straight back into treating him the same way she had treated him when they were teenagers and it was a disorientating experience, but not actively unpleasant, he registered in surprise. There was no awe or flattery, no ego-boosting jokes or flirtatious smiles or carefully choreographed speeches. In the strangest way he found her attitude, her very refusal to be impressed by his status, refreshing.

Later that same day, Jazz got a break at lunchtime. She heaved a sigh over the morning she had endured; lessons had never before made her feel so bored and fed up because all the subject matter was dry as dust. For the first time, however, she was becoming fully aware that Vitale occupied a very different world from her own and the prospect of having to face weeks of such coaching sessions made her wince. But if that was what rescuing her mother demanded from her, she would knuckle down and learn what she had to learn, she conceded reluctantly. A sheaf of supporting notes in front of her, she stroked coloured felt-tipped pens through salient points to highlight them, a practice she had used at university to make reading less of a challenge for her dyslexia. It would be easier for her to ask for spoken notes that she could listen to but she absolutely hated asking for special treatment that drew attention to her learning disability, particularly when it would only remind Vitale of yet another one of her flaws.

Her room, however, was beautiful, she allowed with a rueful smile that took in her silk-clad bed, the polished furniture and the door into the en-suite bathroom. She might as well have been staying in a top-flight exclusive hotel because her surroundings were impossibly luxurious and decidedly in the category of a major treat. The lunch, served in a fancy dining room, had been excellent as well, she was thinking as she sped downstairs for the afternoon session of coaching, wondering what was next on the agenda.

'*Jazz?*' a voice said in disbelief.

Jazz stopped dead mid-flight and stared down at the tall dark man staring up at her from the foyer, swiftly recognising him from his high public profile in the media. 'Angel?' she queried in shock.

'What the hell are you doing in my brother's house?' Angel demanded bluntly, scanning her casual jeans-clad appearance with frowning attention.

Trying to think fast, Jazz descended the stairs, wondering what she was supposed to say to Vitale's half-brother. Were the two men still as close as they had been as kids?

'I think that's a secret so I'd rather not go into detail,' she parried awkwardly. 'How are you?'

'That's OK, Jenkins,' Angel addressed the older man still standing at the front door as if in readiness for the Greek billionaire's departure. 'You can serve coffee in the drawing room for Jazz and I.'

'Where's Vitale?' Jazz enquired nervously.

'Out but we *must* catch up,' Angel said with innate assurance while the older man spread wide the door of what she assumed to be the drawing room.

'Who's Jenkins?' she asked to forestall further questions when the door was closed again.

'Vitale's butler. This is a pretty old-fashioned household,' Angel told her cheerfully. 'Now tell me about the secret because I know my brother better than anyone and Vitale does not *have* secrets.'

'I can't… Don't push me,' Jazz protested in desperation. 'My mother and I are in a bit of a pickle and Vitale is helping us out.'

'Charitable Vitale?' Angel inclined his head thoughtfully. 'Sorry, that doesn't wash.'

'I contacted your father first,' Jazz admitted, hoping that fact would distract him, because Angel was displaying all the characteristics of a terrier on the scent of a juicy bone.

'Tell me about your mother,' Angel invited smoothly.

Jazz gave him a brief résumé of their plight and confided that she had told her family that she was working for Vitale even though she strictly wasn't. 'But if it hadn't been for the *b-bet*—' she stumbled helplessly at letting that word escape '—Vitale wouldn't have needed me in the first place.'

'Bet,' Angel repeated with a sudden flashing smile of triumph. 'Zac, our kid brother, I surmise. And what *is* the bet? Vitale tells me everything.'

And since she had already given away half the story she gave him the whole. Angel gave her a shattered appraisal before he dropped down beside her on the sofa and burst out laughing, so genuinely amused at the prospect of her being coached for a public appearance at a royal ball that she ended up laughing too. Angel had always been so much more down-to-earth than his brother.

That was the point when Vitale entered the room, seeing his brother and Jazz seated close and laughing in a scene of considerable intimacy. That unanticipated sight sent a current of deep-seated rage roaring through Vitale like a hurricane.

'Jazz...you're supposed to be with Jenkins right now, not entertaining my brother!' he bit out rawly, dark golden eyes scorching hot with angry condemnation on her flushed face.

'Jenkins?' she queried, rising upright.

'Table manners,' he extended crushingly, sending a tide of red rushing across her stricken face and not feeling the slightest bit guilty about it.

Jazz fled, mortified that he would say that to her in front of Angel as if she were a half-bred savage, who didn't know how to eat in polite company. Was she? Ridiculous tears prickled at the backs of her eyes and stung. Did Vitale remember her as having had dreadful table manners when she was younger? It was a deeply embarrassing suspicion.

'Well, wasn't that unroyal eruption educational?' Angel quipped as he sprang upright and studied Vitale with a measuring scrutiny. 'Yes, she's turned out quite a looker, our childhood playmate.'

Jazz was only a little soothed to learn that Vitale's butler had been co-opted into teaching her about the right cutlery to use, rather than her manners. Furthermore, for once, she was receiving a lesson she needed, she acknowledged grudgingly, when she was presented with a formal table setting in the dining room that contained a remarkably bewildering choice of knives, forks and spoons. When that was done, she returned to her room and was seated against the headboard, reading a book she had got in a charity shop, when the door opened with an abrupt lack of warning.

It was Vitale and he was furious, as she had never seen him before. A dark flush lay along his high cheekbones, only contriving to accentuate the flaming gold of his spectacular eyes. 'You spilled it all like an oil gusher!' he condemned wrathfully. 'Don't you have any discretion?'

Stiff with discomfiture, Jazz scrambled off the bed in haste. 'I let one word slip and then there didn't seem much point in holding back,' she admitted ruefully. 'I'm sorry if you didn't want him to know.'

'You were too busy flirting with my brother to worry about what you told him!' Vitale accused fiercely.

Jazz was stunned by that interpretation, particularly when her response to Angel had always been more like a sister with a big brother than anything else. She had never felt the smallest spark in Angel's radius, while Vitale could set her on fire with a careless glance. 'I wasn't *flirting* with him!' she replied forcefully. 'That's nonsense.'

'I know what I saw,' Vitale sliced in with contempt. 'You were all over him like a rash!'

Anger began to stir within Jazz as she stared up at Vitale, who was towering over her like a particularly menacing stone wall. 'I didn't even touch him, for goodness' sake! What the hell are you trying to imply?' she demanded.

Already struggling to master a fury unlike any he had ever experienced, Vitale stared down at her, his lean brown hands clenched into fists because he felt incredibly violent. Angel was an incorrigible flirt and women went mad for him. Vitale had never had that freedom, that ready repartee or level of experience, and suddenly that lowering awareness infuriated him. His attention zeroed in on Jazz's luscious pink mouth and suddenly he wanted to taste that mouth so badly it hurt, his body surging in a volatile wave straight from rage to sexual hunger. His brain had nothing to do with that unnerving switch.

Vitale snatched her up off her feet and kissed

her in a move that so disconcerted her she didn't fight, she only gasped. A split second on, the punishing, passionate force of his hard mouth was smashing down on hers, driving her lips apart, his tongue penetrating that moist and sensitive internal space. She shuddered with reaction, her arms balancing on his shoulders, her hands splaying round the back of his neck, fingers delving into the luxuriant depths of his black hair. A tsunami of excitement quivered through Jazz with every deeply sensual plunge of his tongue. It was like nothing she had ever felt in a man's arms before and the very intensity of it was mind-blowing because it was everything she had ever dreamt of and nothing she had ever thought she could feel. He could certainly kiss, she thought helplessly, awash with the stimulation spreading through her heated body.

Without warning, it was over and Vitale was setting her back down on the floor, swinging on his heel and walking out again without a word, even closing the door behind him. Jazz almost laughed, her fingers rising to touch her tingling mouth, wild butterflies unleashed in her tummy. Vitale hadn't said a word, which was *so* typical of him. He would walk away and refuse to think about it or talk about it, as if talking about it would make it more damaging.

But Vitale was genuinely in shock, throbbing with such raw sexual arousal he was in pain, dark golden eyes burning with the self-discipline it had taken to tear himself away. She tasted like strawberries and coffee but she had engulfed him like too much alcohol in his veins. He felt strangely disconnected from himself because his reactions, his very behaviour, were unacceptable and abnormal. He could barely credit that he had been so angry that he had wanted to smash his brother through the wall, couldn't begin to explain what had awakened that anger. He loathed every one of those weird feelings and fought to suppress them and bury them deep. He stripped where he stood in his bedroom before heading for the shower.

In comparison, Jazz lay on top of her very comfortable bed and thought about that kiss, the ultimate kiss, which had shot her full of adrenalin, excitement and longing. She felt as if she had been waiting half her life to discover that a kiss could make her feel like that, but it was a terrible disappointment that Vitale had achieved that feat because there would be no interesting future developments happening in that quarter, she reflected wryly. It was just sex, stupid, confusing sexual urges that had neither sense nor staying power, and she should write it off to a silly impulse and a moment of forgetfulness. He wasn't even the sort of guy she wanted in her life and he never would be. He was too arrogant, too reserved, too quick to judge…but, my goodness, he knew how to kiss…

Fate had short-changed her, she thought resentfully. She was still a virgin because she had always been waiting to meet a man, who would make her crave more of his touch. She had wanted her first lover to be someone whom she desired and cared about. Unfortunately, desire had evaded her in the invasive groping sessions that had been her sad experience as a student.

Even worse, she still remembered the emotional hurt inflicted by her father's abuse. How could she trust any man when her own father had attacked her? Jazz had been wary of the opposite sex ever since, even though she was now wishing she had a little more sexual experience because then she would have had a better idea of how to read Vitale and deal with him.

Had her crush on Vitale at fourteen made her more vulnerable? Jazz cringed at the suspicion and dismissed it because she hadn't actively thought about Vitale in years and years. He had only come to mind when she'd seen him in some glossy magazine, squiring some equally superior beauty at some sparkling celebrity event and, like Cinderella in real life, she thought sadly, she had known how impossible her dream had been at fourteen. He was what he was: a prince, born and bred to a life so different from hers that he might as well have been an alien from another planet. He wasn't a *happy* prince either, she thought with unwilling compassion. Even as an adolescent she had recognised that Vitale didn't really know what being happy was.

When she was informed that she had another coaching session late that afternoon, she was incensed to learn that it was in deportment. She put in the time with the instructor and then knocked on Vitale's office door.

'Yes?' Vitale looked up from his laptop and then sprang upright with the perfect courtesy that was engrained in him. Woman enters room: *stand*, she reflected ruefully, and it took just a little bit of the edge off her temper and the faint unease she had felt at seeing him again so soon after that kiss. It definitely didn't help, though, that he still looked gorgeous to her from the head of his slightly ruffled black hair down to his wonderful dark deep-set eyes that even now were clearly registering wariness. She knew exactly what he was thinking and almost grinned. He was still waiting to be attacked over the kiss.

'Deportment?' she queried drily instead. 'Don't you think that's overkill? I don't slouch and I can walk in a straight line in heels. What more do you want?'

His dark eyes flared gold and he tensed, reining back all that leaping energy of his. 'I thought it might be necessary but if it's not—'

'It's not,' Jazz cut in combatively.

'Then we can wave goodbye to that session,' Vitale conceded mildly, watching her walk across his office to look out of the window. She was wearing that damnably ugly skirt and heels again, but had he been of a literary bent he could have written a poem along the lines of what that cheap fabric did to the curve of her little rounded bottom where he had had both hands clasped only hours earlier. It had felt every bit as good and femininely lush as it looked, he acknowledged, thoroughly unsettled by that thought and the pulse at his groin. The effect she had on his body was like a kind of madness, he decided then in consternation.

'I have some questions about this bet and you may not think I'm entitled to answers,' Jazz remarked stiffly. 'Who are you planning to say I am at the ball?'

His winged ebony brows drew together in bewilderment. 'What do you mean?'

Jazz threw her shoulders back. 'Well, I assumed you'd be giving me a fake name.'

Vitale frowned, currently engaged in noticing how red and full her lips seemed, wondering if he had been rough because he had *felt* rough, drunk on lust and need, out of control. 'Why would I give you a fake name?'

'Because if I'm pictured with you anywhere the press might go digging and wouldn't they just love pointing out that the Prince has a housekeeper's daughter on his arm?' Jazz extended stiffly, gooseflesh rising in the claustrophobic atmosphere and the intensity of his gaze.

'*So?*' Vitale prompted thickly, acknowledging that kissing her had been one of the most exhilarating encounters he had ever had and cringing at the awareness. He was an adult man with a great sex life, he reminded himself doggedly. As Angel would say, he really needed to get out more.

'Doesn't that bother you?' Jazz asked in surprise.

'No. Why would it? I'm not foisting a fake personality or some sort of scam on the public. This bet is for private consumption only,' Vitale explained. 'There's nothing wrong with being a housekeeper's daughter.'

'No, there's not,' Jazz agreed with the glimmerings of her first real smile in his presence and the startling realisation that Vitale was not quite the snob she had believed he was. It was as if a giant defensive barrier inside her dropped and, disturbed by the discovery, she quickly turned to leave him alone again.

'Jazz…once you get clothes delivered tomorrow we'll be going out to dinner in the evening,' Vitale informed her, startling her even more. 'Your first public appearance.'

Dining out with Vitale, Jazz ruminated in wonder as she returned to her room, planning an evening composed of a long luxurious bath, washing her hair and watching something on TV.

CHAPTER FOUR

JAZZ COULDN'T SLEEP. Accustomed to a much more physically active existence, she wasn't tired and at two in the morning she put the light back on and tried to read until hunger took over and consumed her. She knew she shouldn't but she loved a slice of toast and a hot drink before bed and the longer she lay awake, the more all-consuming the craving became. Inevitably she got up, raising her brows at her appearance in the faded long tee shirt she wore to bed. No dressing gown, no slippers in her wardrobe but so what? If she was quiet she doubted if she would wake up the very correct Jenkins.

The stairs creaked and she didn't like moving round in total darkness but a light could rouse someone likely to investigate. By touch she located the door at the back of the hall and through that a flight of stairs, which ran down into the basement area where she assumed the kitchen lay. Safely through that door, she put on lights and relaxed. The kitchen was as massive as a hotel kitchen and she padded about on the cold tiles, trying not to shiver. She located bread and the toaster and milk and then, wonder of wonders, some hot-chocolate powder to make her favourite night-time drink. Jazz was grateful she wasn't like her aunt, who joked that she only had to look at a bar of chocolate to gain an inch on her hips.

Her toast ready, she sat down at the table to eat with appetite, eyes closing blissfully as she munched hot butter-laden toast, which was the first glimpse Vitale had of her as he strode barefoot through the door.

'You can't wander round here in the middle of the night!' he began impatiently. 'My security team wakened me.'

'Your security... *What?*' Jazz gasped, startled out of her life by the interruption and even more startled by the vision Vitale made bare-chested and barefoot, clad only in a pair of tight jeans. He was completely transformed by casual clothing, she conceded in awe.

Vitale groaned out loud. 'The whole house is wired with very sensitive security equipment and I have a full team of bodyguards who monitor it.'

'But I didn't see anything and no alarm went off.'

'It's composed of invisible beams and it's silent. As soon as the team established that it wasn't an intrusion but a member of the household they contacted me, not wishing to frighten you.'

'Well, I'm not frightened of you,' she mumbled round a mouthful of toast that she was trying to masticate enough not to choke when she swallowed because, in reality, Vitale was delicious shorn of his shirt and her mouth had gone all dry.

He was a classic shape, all broad shoulders, rippling muscular torso sprinkled with dark curls of hair leading down into a vee at his hips and a flat, taut stomach. Clothed she could just about contrive to resist him, half-naked he was an intolerable lure to her eyes.

'They saw you on camera, realised that you weren't fully dressed and surmised that the sudden intrusion of a strange man could scare you.'

'On *camera*?' she repeated in horror, striving to recall if she had scratched or done anything inappropriate while she was in the kitchen, bracing her hands on the table top to rise to her feet and move away from it.

Vitale shifted lean dark hands upward in a soothing motion. 'Relax, they've all been switched off. We're not being monitored right now.'

'Thank goodness for that,' she framed tremulously, the perky tips of her nipples pushing against the tee shirt below Vitale's riveted gaze. 'I only got up to get something to eat.'

'That's perfectly all right,' Vitale assured her thickly, inwardly speculating on whether she was wearing anything at all below the nightshirt or whatever it was. 'But for the future, I'll show you a button you can press just to let security know someone's wandering around the house and this won't happen again.'

'OK,' Jazz muttered, still shaken up at the idea that she had been watched without her knowledge by strange men.

Vitale ran a surprisingly gentle hand down the side of her downturned face. 'It's not a problem. You haven't done anything wrong,' he murmured sibilantly, his accent catching along the edges of his dark, deep, masculine voice.

A shocking flare of heat rose up from the heart of her as he touched her face and Jazz threw her head back in mortification, her green eyes wide with diluted pupils.

'Don't look at me like that,' Vitale framed hoarsely. 'You have the most beautiful eyes… You always did. And I didn't intend to say that, don't know which random brain cell it came from.'

An overpowering need to smile tilted Jazz's tense lips because he sounded so stressed and so confounded by his own words. Beautiful eyes, well, that was something, her first and probably only ever compliment from Vitale, who worked so hard at keeping his distance. But he had touched her first, she reminded herself with faint pride in what felt vaguely like an achievement. Her body was taut as a bowstring and breathing was a major challenge as she looked up into dark, smouldering golden intensity. Ditto, beautiful eyes, she labelled, but she didn't really think women were supposed to say things like that to men so she kept quiet out of fear that he would laugh.

'*Troppa fantasia...* I have too much imagination,' Vitale breathed, being steadily ripped in two by the conflicting impulses yanking at him. He knew he should let her go and return to bed but he didn't want to. He was ridiculously fascinated that, even in the middle of the night and fresh from her bed with tousled hair, she looked fantastic. And so very different from the women he was used to, women who went to bed in make-up and rose before him to put on another face to greet the dawn, and his awakening, plastic perfect, contrived, artificial, everything that Jazz was not. Jazz was *real* right down to her little naturally pink toenails and that trait was incredibly attractive to him. With Jazz what you saw was literally what you got and there were no pitfalls of strategy or seduction lined up to trip him.

'I would never have thought it,' Jazz almost whispered, so painfully conscious of his proximity that the little hairs were rising on the back of her neck. 'You're a banker.'

'And I can't have an imagination too?' Vitale inserted with a sudden flashing smile of amusement that would have knocked for six the senses of a stronger woman than Jazz.

'It's unexpected,' she mumbled uncertainly, all of a quiver in receipt of that mesmerising, almost boyish grin. 'You always seem so serious.'

'I don't feel serious around you,' Vitale admitted, tiring of looking down at her and getting a crick in his neck. In a sudden movement that took her very much by surprise, he bent, closed his hands to her tiny waist and lifted her up. He settled her down on the end of the table. He was incredibly, ferociously aroused but Jazz seemed curiously unaware of the chemistry between them, almost innocent. No way could she be *that* innocent, he told himself urgently, because he would never touch an innocent woman and he desperately needed to touch her. His lovers were always experienced women, who knew the score.

'But then you never know what you're feeling,' Jazz quipped. 'You're not into self-analysis.'

'How do you know that?' Vitale demanded with a frown.

'I see it in you,' Jazz told him casually.

Vitale didn't like the conversation, didn't want to talk either. He spread his hands to either side of her triangular face and he tasted that alluring pink mouth with unashamed passion.

Jazz was afraid her heart was about to leap right out of her chest, her breathlessness as physical as her inability to think that close to him. She felt nebulously guilty, as if on some level her brain was striving to warn her that she was doing something wrong, but she absolutely refused to listen to that message when excitement was rushing like fire through her nerve endings. Her nipples tightened, her slender thighs pushing firmly together on the embarrassing dampness gathering at the apex of her legs.

'*Per l'amor di Dio...*' Vitale swore, fighting for control because he was already aching. 'What do you do to me?'

'What *do* I do to you?' Jazz whispered, full of curiosity.

She excited the hell out of him but he was too experienced to let that salient fact drop from his lips. 'You tempt me beyond my control,' Vitale heard himself admit regardless and was shocked by the reality.

'That's all right,' Jazz breezed, one hand smoothing up over a high cheekbone, the roughness of his stubbled jaw lending a brooding darkness to his lean, strong face in the dimly lit kitchen, her other hand tracing an exploring path up over the sweep of his long, smooth back. 'Are you sure those cameras are all off?' she framed, peering anxiously round the brightly lit kitchen.

'*All* of them,' Vitale stressed, but he strode back to the door to douse the strong overhead illumination, plunging them into a much more welcoming and more intimate space only softly lit by the lights below the cupboards.

Her hand slid back to his spine. His skin was hot, faintly damp but it was his eyes she was watching and thinking about, those beautiful black-fringed eyes singing a clear song of stress and bewilderment and the glorious liberating message that he wasn't any more in charge of what was happening between them than she was.

'I want you, *bellezza mia*,' he growled all soft and rough, sending shimmying awareness right down her taut spine just as he reached down and lifted her tee shirt and whipped it off over her head.

Jazz loosed a startled yelp and almost whipped her hands up to cover her naked body, but in that same split second of dismay she asked herself if she wanted to be a virgin for ever and if she would ever have the chance to have such a skilled lover, as Vitale was almost certain to be, again. And the answer to both questions was no. He wasn't going to want a shy woman, was he?

And he had to know all the right moves to ensure the experience was good for her, hadn't he?

'You are *so* beautiful,' Vitale almost crooned, his hands rising to cup her delicate little breasts, which were topped with taut rosy tips that he stroked appreciatively with his thumb.

And that fast, Jazz had no desire to either cover up or breathe because the fabulous joy and satisfaction of being deemed beautiful by Vitale overwhelmed her. In gratitude, she stretched up to find his mouth again for herself, nibbling at his lower lip, circling slowly with newly discovered sensuality while all the time he was stroking and rolling and squeezing the peaks of her breasts that she had never known could be so responsive to a man's touch. Little fiery arrows were travelling down to the heart of her, making her hips shift and squirm on the table as the heat and tightness increased there. And then, with what felt like very little warning to her, a climax shot through her like an electric charge, making her cry out in surprise and pleasure.

'And as responsive as my most erotic dream,' Vitale husked, wrenching at the zip of his jeans.

A lean brown hand pried her legs apart while she was still in a sort of blissful cocoon of reaction. Vitale pulled her closer and tipped her back to facilitate his intentions. A long finger traced her entrance and eased inside. He uttered a hungry groan of appreciation because she was very wet and tight and then he froze. 'I'll have to take you upstairs to get a condom,' he bit out in frustration.

'I'm on birth control,' Jazz muttered helpfully. 'But are you…safe?'

'Yes because I've never had sex without a condom,' Vitale confided, but the temptation to try it without that barrier was huge. He tried to argue with himself but, poised between her legs, craving the welcome her slender, lithe body offered his raging arousal, he realised it was a lost battle for him before it even started.

With strong hands he eased her closer still and she felt him, hard and demanding against her most tender flesh, and both nerves and eagerness assailed her. Her whole body came alive with electrified longing as if that first redemptive taste of pleasure had ignited an unquenchable fire of need inside her. He sank into her by easy degrees, groaning something out loud in Italian as she buried her face against a satin-smooth brown shoulder, barely crediting she was making love with Vitale, every sense she possessed rioting with sensation, the very smell and taste of his skin thrilling her.

And then he slammed right to the heart of her and a stinging pain made her grit her teeth and jerk in reaction. Withdrawing a little, Vitale paused for an instant, pushing up her face and looking down at her with what appeared to be brazen incredulity, and she knew then that at the very least he suspected he had been her first lover and he wasn't pleased. But she ignored that unwelcome suspicion and wriggled her hips with feminine encouragement, watching him react and groan with a newly learned sense of empowerment.

'Don't stop,' she told him.

And for the very first time ever, Vitale did exactly as she told him. He sank deeper again, stretching the tender walls of her heated core with hungry thoroughness and, that instant of pain forgotten, Jazz craved his contact. He gave her more, picking up speed, hard and fast until he was pounding into her and her excitement climbed with his every fluid, forceful thrust. It was much wilder and infinitely more uninhibited than she had dimly expected from a man as reserved as Vitale; indeed it was passionately explosive. She reached another climax and her body convulsed around his, the whole world, it seemed, erupting around her as he shot her into a deeply erotic and exhilarating release. A faint ache pulled at her as he withdrew and zipped his jeans.

'Diavolo!' Vitale exclaimed, stepping back from her while she fumbled for her tee shirt and hurriedly pulled it on over her head with hands that felt clumsy and unable to do her bidding. 'Why the hell didn't you tell me you were a virgin?'

Fixing her face to a determined blank, Jazz slid off the table, only just resisting a revealing moan as discomfort travelled through her lower body. 'We're not having a post-mortem,' she parried sharply, mortification engulfing her in an unanticipated tide that threatened to drown her. 'You're not entitled to ask nosy questions.'

She had had sex on a kitchen table with Vitale and she couldn't quite believe it but she certainly knew she didn't intend to linger to discuss it!

For a split second of frustration, Vitale wanted to strangle her. Her hectically flushed face was mutinous and furious and she was pointedly avoiding looking at him, which annoyed the hell out of him even though he didn't understand why. After all, he didn't want a post-mortem either, didn't have a clue why or how what they had just done had happened and could think of at least ten good reasons why it *shouldn't* have happened.

He watched her limp across the tiled floor as if she had had a run-in with a bus instead of her first experience of sex and he felt hellishly guilty and responsible. He experienced a sudden, even more startling desire to scoop her up and sink her into a warm reviving bath…and then have sex with her again? As if that were likely to improve anything, he reflected sardonically, raking unsteady fingers through his tousled black hair. What the hell was wrong with him? His brain was all over the place and he couldn't think straight but he knew he had just enjoyed the best sex of his life and that was downright terrifying…

Jazz had informed Vitale that there would be no post-mortem but, seated in a bath at three in the morning, Jazz was unhappily engaged in staging her own. Had she actually thought of what they had done as 'making love'? Yes, she had and she was so ashamed of herself for that fanciful label because she really wasn't *that* naïve. It had been sex, pure and simple, and she knew the difference because she wasn't a dreamy teenager any longer, she was an adult. Or *supposed* to be, she thought with tears stinging the backs of her eyes and regret digging wires of steel through her shrinking body.

Of course, they would both pretend it hadn't happened…a moment of madness, the mistake swiftly buried and forgotten. After all, this was Vitale she was dealing with and he wasn't going to want to talk about it either. On that front, therefore, she was safe, she assured herself soothingly. It was his fault in any case—he had had no business parading around half-naked in jeans and tempting her into that insanity. She hugged her knees in the warm water and sighed. She had done a stupid, stupid thing and now she had to live with it and with Vitale for weeks and weeks, being all polite and standoffish, lest he think she was up for a repeat encounter. Running away or hiding wasn't an option.

A knock sounded lightly on the door and she almost reared out of the bath in her horror because she abruptly appreciated that Vitale was *not* running true to form. In a blind panic she snatched at a towel and wrapped it round her, opening the door the merest chink to say discouragingly, 'Yes?'

Vitale discovered that he was immediately possessed by an impossibly strong urge to smash the door down and he gritted his teeth on yet another unfamiliar prompting to act unreasonably and violently. 'Will you please come out? You have been in there for ages.'

From that point he wasn't the only individual valiantly gritting teeth. Her flushed face frozen as he had never seen it before, Jazz emerged from the bathroom, noting that he had put on a black shirt. 'I didn't know you were waiting,' she said dulcetly, leaning heavily on her one and only elocution lesson.

'Look, don't go all girlie on me. I don't expect that from you,' Vitale countered crushingly. 'I only want the answer to one question.'

Jazz tried to unfreeze a little and look normal, or as normal as she could feel being confronted by Vitale when she was wearing only a towel. 'OK.'

'Why is a virgin on birth control?' he asked gravely.

'I don't really think that's any of your business. It was for…well, medical reasons,' she told him obliquely, unwilling to discuss her menstrual cycle with him, her colour heightening until she felt like a beetroot being roasted and wanted to slap him for it.

'It will be very much my business if you get pregnant,' Vitale breathed witheringly.

'It's so like you to look on the dark side and expect the very worst,' Jazz replied equally witheringly. 'It's not going to happen, Vitale. Relax and go back to bed and please forget this ever happened for both our sakes.'

'Is that what you want?' Vitale wanted to rip off the towel and continue even though he knew she was in no condition to satisfy him again. It had nothing whatsoever to do with his brain. It was pretty much as if his body had developed an agenda all of its own and he couldn't control it.

'We just had a sleazy encounter on a kitchen table in the middle of the night. What do you think?' Jazz enquired saccharine sweet.

Vitale was receiving a strong impression that anything he said would be taken down and held against him. *Sleazy?* That single descriptive word outraged him. He swung on his heel, his lean, powerful body taut, and left the room and just as quickly Jazz wanted to kick him for giving up on her so easily. Her thoughts were a turbulent sea of conflict and confusion and self-loathing, sending her seesawing from one extreme to the other. No sooner was he gone than she wanted him back and she flung off the towel and climbed into bed, hating herself. It was so typical of Vitale to worry about the fact that he hadn't used contraception. Now he would be waiting on that axe to fall and that was a humiliating prospect, even though it also reminded her that she hadn't yet taken her daily pill. She dug into her bag and took it before switching off the light.

What was done was done and it had been amazing, she thought ruefully, but it was better not to think about that imprudent sudden intimacy that had changed everything between them. Now she was no longer thinking about Vitale as the boy he had once been, but Vitale, very much a man in the present and that switch in outlook disturbed her, made her fear that somewhere deep down inside her there was still a tiny kernel of the four-teen-year-old who had believed the sun rose and set on Prince Vitale Castiglione...

CHAPTER FIVE

'WOMEN MY AGE don't wear clothes like this,' Jazz was saying by late morning the next day, appalled by the vast collection of garments, all distinguished solely by their lack of personality. 'I'm not your future wife or one of your relatives. I'm supposed to be only a girlfriend. Why would I be dressed like an older woman?'

'I want you to be elegant,' Vitale responded, unimpressed by her reasoning. He wanted every bit of her covered up. He didn't want her showing off her shapely legs or her fabulous figure for other men to drool over. Recognising Angel's appreciation of the beauty Jazz had become had been quite sufficient warning on that score. 'I imagine you would prefer to show more flesh.'

That was the last straw for Jazz after a trying few hours of striving to behave normally when she did see Vitale between coaching sessions. Temper pushed up through her like lava seeking a crack to escape. 'Where do you get all these prejudices about me from?' she demanded hotly. 'I don't wear revealing clothes. I never have. And as you know I haven't got much to reveal!'

'You have more than enough for me, *bellezza mia*,' Vitale breathed half under his breath, heat stirring at his groin as he thought about the delectable little swells he had explored the night before.

Jazz flinched and acted studiously deaf in receipt of that tactless reminder. He was no good at pretending, she recognised ruefully. 'This stuff is all so bland,' she complained instead, fingering a pair of tailored beige trousers with a curled lip. There was a lot of beige, a lot of navy and a lot of brown. He was even biased against bright colour. 'If this is your taste, you certainly didn't miss out on a chance of fame in the fashion industry.'

Vitale reached a decision and signalled the stylist waiting at the far end of the very large room.

'Miss Dickens is in charge of the selections. By the sound of it, she will be ordering a more adventurous wardrobe,' he declared, watching the slow smile that lit up Jazz's piquant little face while smoothly congratulating himself on knowing when to ease up on exerting control. 'But pick out something here to wear tonight.'

Jazz chose a fitted navy dress and shoes and lingerie as well as a bag.

'Thanks!' she called in Vitale's wake as he left her alone with the stylist to share her own likes and dislikes.

His arrogant dark head turned in acknowledgement, brilliant dark-fringed eyes a fiery gold enticement, and desire punched her so hard in the chest that she paled, stricken that she could have made herself so vulnerable. Putting such pointless thoughts from her mind, she concentrated on choosing clothes and particularly on the necessary selection of a spectacular gown for the royal ball.

After asking for lunch to be served in her room she was free to go home and visit her family for a few hours, and it was a welcome break from the hothouse atmosphere of Vitale's imposing London home. Her mother and her aunt were baking and Jazz sat down with a cup of tea and tried to feel normal again.

But she didn't feel normal after she had put on the navy dress over the silk lingerie, her feet shod in hand-stitched leather sandals with smart heels. Although she had never bothered much with make-up she made a special effort with mascara and lipstick, knowing that that was one thing she did need that Vitale probably hadn't thought about: make-up lessons.

'No, I like you the way you are,' Vitale asserted, startling her in the limo on the way out to dinner. 'Natural, healthy. You have beautiful skin... Why cover it?'

Jazz shifted an uncertain shoulder. 'Because it's what women do... They make the most of themselves.'

Vitale studied her from his corner of the limo. She looked stunning, the dark dress throwing her amazing hair into prominence and emphasising her delicate figure and long slender legs. He willed his arousal to subside because he had made decisions earlier that day. He was going to step back, play safe, ensure that there was no more sex, no more blurring of the lines between them, but he only had to look at her to find his resolution wavering.

That had never happened to Vitale before with a woman. He had never succumbed to an infatuation, had always assumed that he simply wasn't the emotional type. His affairs were always cool and sexual, nothing extra required or needed on either side. Naturally he had been warned since he was a teenager that he would, in all likelihood, have to marry for dynastic reasons rather than love and he had always guarded himself on the emotional front. What he felt for Jazz was desire, irresistible burning desire, and there was no great mystery about that when it was simply hormones, he told himself soothingly.

A current of discreetly turned heads and a low buzz of comment surrounded their passage to their table in the wildly exclusive restaurant where they were to dine. Vitale's gaze glittered like black diamonds when he saw other men directing lustful looks at Jazz. For the moment, Jazz was *his*, absolutely his, whether he was having sex with her or otherwise, he reasoned stubbornly.

Jazz sat down, surveying the table to become belatedly grateful for Jenkins's lesson in cutlery clarification. 'So, tell me what you've been doing since you left school?' she invited him cheerfully. 'Apart from being a prince and all that.'

They talked about being students. Vitale admitted that banking had been the only viable option for him. He also told her that he had a house in Italy where he planned to take her before the ball.

'For how long?' she asked, her lovely face pensive in the candlelight, which picked up every fiery hue in her multi-shaded red mane of hair for his appreciation. 'I like to see my mother regularly.'

'A couple of weeks, no more. When this is over, *after* the ball—' Vitale shifted a fluid, lean brown hand in emphasis '—I will pay for you to finish your degree so that you can work in your chosen field.'

'That's a very generous offer but you're already covering quite enough in the financial line,' she began in surprise and some embarrassment.

'No. I tricked you,' Vitale divulged, disconcerting her even more with that abrupt confession of wrongdoing. 'My father is settling your mother's loans. He wanted to. It makes him feel that he has helped her.'

'You...*tricked*...me?' Jazz gasped in disbelief that he could quietly admit that.

'Being a bastard comes naturally. I needed you to accept the bet and I used *your* need for money to win your agreement,' Vitale pointed out levelly. 'I feel that I owe you that amount of honesty because you have been honest with me.'

'So, you're saying your father would *always* have helped?' Jazz prodded in even greater surprise because she wasn't, once she thought about it, that shocked to discover that Vitale could be extremely calculating and shrewd. She didn't, however, feel that she was in a position to complain or protest because if he had used her to suit his own purposes, she was also most assuredly using *him*. Having already received a discreet cheque in payment for her supposed salary, she had given it in its entirety to her mother. No, she wasn't proud that she had accepted money from a man she had also slept with, but she really could not bear to watch her mother scrimp and struggle. Being seriously poor had taught Jazz a lot of tough life lessons.

'Papa feels very guilty about your mother. He was concerned that there was a possibility of domestic abuse in your parents' marriage...' Vitale volunteered very quietly after their plates had been cleared away.

Jazz turned sheet white and her fingers curled into the tablecloth, scrunching it. 'There was,' she conceded, thrown back in time to a period she rarely revisited. 'My father was violent when life didn't go his way and he took it out on us.'

Vitale was appalled and then shocked that he was appalled because he had heard of such situations, but then he had never personally known anyone who confessed to being a victim of domestic abuse. 'You…as well as your mother?'

'On several occasions when I tried to protect Mum. Poor Mum got the worst of it,' Jazz conceded heavily. 'Dad was hooked on online gambling and when he lost money he took it out on his family with his fists.'

A very real stab of anger coursed through Vitale at that news. He was remembering Jazz as a tiny child and a skinny teen and realising that she knew what it was to live in fear within a violent home where she should have been safe. His strong jawline was rigid. 'I'm sorry you had to go through that experience.'

Jazz pursed her lips and sighed. 'I think that was why Mum ran off with her second husband, Jeff. He was supposed to be her escape but he was more of a dead end. He wasn't violent, just dishonest. But you know, the older I get, the more I realise that many people have had bad experiences when they were young,' she told him in an upbeat tone. 'It doesn't have to define you and it doesn't have to hold you back and make you distrust everyone you meet. You can move beyond it. I know I have.'

Vitale stretched out a hand and squeezed hers to make her release the tablecloth and she laughed and let go of it when she appreciated what she had been doing, her lack of self-pity and her strength delighting him.

'I have the mother from hell,' he confessed unexpectedly. 'Controlling, domineering, very nasty. If she has a heart, I've never seen it. All she cares about is the Lerovian throne and all the pomp and ceremony that go with it.'

Jazz smiled, pleased that he trusted her enough to admit that. 'You're very lucky to have such a pleasant father, then,' she pointed out.

'Sì...' Vitale confirmed, startled that he had spoken ill of his mother for the first time ever and quite unable to explain where those disloyal words had come from. There was something odd about Jazz that provoked him into acting against his own nature, he decided darkly. Maybe it was simply the fact that she was so relaxed in his company that she broke through his reserve. Was that why he was acting out of character?

As for the problem that was his mother, he had only told the truth, he reasoned ruefully. Sofia Castiglione was feared even by the royal household. It was not disloyalty to tell the truth, he acknowledged then, while marvelling that in admitting that salient fact to Jazz he felt some of his tension drop away.

Outside the restaurant, the limousine awaited them, two security guards forcing a man with a camera to back off. The flash of a photo being taken momentarily blinded her as Vitale guided her at speed back into the limo.

'Who is she?' another voice shouted.

'Who am I?' she teased Vitale with amusement as she settled back into her seat.

'A mystery redhead. I will not give out your name. I have no intention of doing the work of the paparazzi for them,' Vitale supplied, his attention locked to her small, vivid face, so pale against the backdrop of that mass of vibrant hair, fine freckles scattered across her diminutive nose.

Hands off, he reminded himself doggedly even as he ached.

'Do you want a drink?' he enquired as they entered the house.

'No, thanks. I'm sort of tired,' she admitted, because she had had little sleep the night before, but she was not about to allude to that reality when Vitale was behaving like a perfect gentleman who had never once touched her. 'Goodnight.'

She kicked off her shoes inside her room, feeling oddly lonely, and wriggled down the zip on her dress to peel it off and hang it up with the care demanded by a superior garment. She stripped and freshened up before reaching for the silky robe she had taken from the clothes selection earlier that day and that was when someone rapped on the door and it opened almost simultaneously.

Vitale strode in, leant back against the door to close it again and said thickly, 'I don't want to say goodnight...'

Surprised in the act of frantically tying the sash on her robe closed, Jazz literally stopped breathing. Smouldering dark golden eyes assailed hers in an almost physical assault and her heart started banging inside her chest like a drum. 'But we—'

'We are both single, free to do whatever we like,' Vitale incised, suppressing every thought he had had, every decision he had made only hours earlier in favour of surrendering to the hunger that had flamed up inside him the instant she'd tried to walk away from him.

Air bubbled back into her lungs and she snatched in a sudden deep breath. *'But,'* she started afresh, inexplicably feeling that *she* had to be the voice of reason.

Vitale prowled forward with the grace of a jungle cat. 'Is there anyone else in your life?'

'Of course not. If there had been, last night wouldn't have happened,' she protested.

'Then I don't see a problem, *bellezza mia,*' Vitale proclaimed in a roughened undertone as he teased loose the knot in the sash in a very slow way. 'Let's keep it simple.'

Simple? But it *wasn't* simple, she wanted to scream while knowing that he was taking his time with the sash to give her the opportunity to say no if she wanted to. But she didn't want to say no, didn't want him to leave her again and that disturbing awareness shook her up. Her heart was thumping so hard she could've been in the last stage of running a marathon and all she could see was Vitale ahead of her, those scorching dark golden eyes with a black fringe of gold-tipped lush lashes that a supermodel would have envied. Somehow, *he* was her finishing line and she couldn't fight that, didn't have that amount of resistance when he was right there in front of her, wanting her, *needing* her, Jazmine Dickens, against all the odds…

He eased the robe off her slight shoulders and let it drop and when her hands whipped up to cover herself, he groaned and forestalled her, trapping her small hands in his. 'I want to see you, *all* of you.'

Her hands fell away, green eyes wide with uncertainty, and he lifted her up, threw back the covers on the bed and laid her down.

'You're wearing too many clothes,' she told him shakily.

Vitale dealt her a slanting grin that lit up his lean, darkly handsome features like the sunrise. He undressed with almost military precision, stowing cuff links by the bed, stacking his suit on a chair, peeling off snug black briefs that could barely contain his urgent arousal. A slow burn ignited in her pelvis, her nipples tinging into tight buds, a melting sensation warming between her thighs.

It was only sex, she bargained fiercely with the troubled thoughts she was refusing to acknowledge, only sex and lots of people had sex simply for fun. She could be the same, she swore to herself, she would *not* make the mistake of believing that what they had was anything more serious than a casual affair. That was what Vitale had meant when he said, 'Let's keep it simple...'

He joined her on the bed, all hair-roughened brown skin and rippling muscle, so wonderfully, fundamentally different from hers, the sexual allure of his body calling to her as much as her body seemed to call to him. He kissed her and the fireworks started inside her, heat and longing rising exponentially with every searing dip of his tongue inside the moist interior of her mouth.

Her entire body felt sensitised, on an edge of unbearable anticipation.

'I want to show you the way it should have been last night,' Vitale husked. 'Last night was rough and ready.'

'But it worked,' she mumbled unevenly, running a forefinger along the wide sensual line of his lips, revelling in the freedom to do so.

'You deserve more,' Vitale insisted, bending his arrogant dark head to catch a swollen pink nipple in his mouth and tease it. 'Much more...'

And much more was very much what she got as Vitale worked a purposeful passage down over her slender length, pausing in places she hadn't even known had nerve endings and dallying there until she was writhing in abandonment, before finally settling between her spread thighs and addressing his attention to the most sensitive place of all.

Self-consciousness was drowned by excitement, sheer physical excitement that she could not restrain. He used his mouth on her, circling, flicking, working her body as though it were an instrument and her pleasure grew by tormentingly sweet degrees until the tightness banding her pelvis became a formless, overwhelming need she could no longer withstand. When he traced the entrance to her lush opening, her spine arched and she cried out as a drowning flood of pleasure surged through her slight body and left her limp.

'Much better,' Vitale pronounced hoarsely, staring down at her enraptured expression with satisfaction. 'That's how it should have been the first time and if you'd warned me—'

'You probably wouldn't have continued,' Jazz interrupted, tying him back down to earth again with that frank assessment.

'You don't know that,' Vitale argued fierily, pushing back her slim thighs and sliding between them, the urgency in his lean, strong body unashamed.

Jazz looked up at him, wondering how she knew it, but know it she did even though it wasn't very diplomatic to drop it on him like that when he was so hopeless at grasping the way his own mind worked. 'I suspected it,' she admitted.

'Nothing short of an earthquake would have stopped me last night!' Vitale swore vehemently, finally surging into her moist, tender sheath with a bone-deep groan of appreciation. 'You feel glorious, *bellezza mia...*'

And the powerful surge of his thick, rigid length into her sensitive core felt equally glorious to Jazz, stretching the inner walls, filling her tight. Her eyes closed and her head rolled back on the pillow as she let the pulsing pleasure consume her. Ripples of delight quivered through her and she arched up her hips, helpless in the grip of her need. Nothing had ever felt so right or so necessary to her. He ground his body into hers and she saw stars behind her lowered eyelids. She began to move against him, hot and frenzied as he slammed into her, primal excitement seizing her with his heart thundering over hers. And then she reached a ravishing peak and rhythmic convulsions clenched her womb as he shuddered over her with an uninhibited shout of satisfaction. A rush of sensation washed her away in the aftermath of lingering pleasure.

'It's amazing with you,' Vitale gritted breathlessly, releasing her from his weight.

Jazz stretched out her arms and tried to snatch him back. 'Don't move away.'

'I'm not into hugging.'

'Tough,' Jazz told him, snuggling up to him regardless. 'I need hugs.'

Vitale's big body literally froze, tested out of his comfort zone.

'It's called compromise and we are all capable of it,' Jazz muttered drowsily against his chest, one arm anchoring round him like an imprisoning chain. 'I'm not telling you I love you because I *don't*. I'm just fond of you, so don't make a fuss about nothing.'

In a quandary, Vitale, who had been planning to return to his own room, lay staring up at the ceiling. He had to stretch away from her to switch off the light, but she hooked him back with the efficiency of a retriever picking up game even though from the sound of her even breathing he knew she was definitely asleep.

She was so blunt, he reflected helplessly, wondering if he should simply push her away to make it back to his own bed. He was relieved that she had no evident illusions about their relationship and wasn't thinking along the lines of love because he didn't want to hurt her. Seducing a virgin was a dangerous game, he acknowledged, wondering why she had still been untouched, wondering why he was even interested because his interest in his lovers was usually very superficial. He didn't quite know how he had ended up having sex with her again and wondered if it mattered. He decided it didn't and if he slept with her, he could have her again in the morning, so staying put made very good sense...

'Could we just rough it for a night?' Jazz asked hopefully a week later.

Vitale frowned. 'Rough it?'

'Instead of going to some very fancy restaurant, we could go to a supper club I know that does ethnic dishes. It's cheap but the food's great.' Studying his unenthusiastic expression, Jazz grimaced. 'Vitale, just for once can we go off the official map?'

'I don't follow an official map,' Vitale argued, meeting hopeful eyes and simply wanting to see the liveliness return to her lovely face, which was telegraphing her conviction that he would refuse her suggestion. 'All right, just this once but if either of us get food poisoning, you're dead!'

'We're not going to get food poisoning,' she assured him with a confident grin.

They ate a delicious and surprisingly elaborate five-course meal in a private city garden and Vitale drank out of a bottle without complaint and watched Jazz sparkle across the table. He was more relaxed than he could ever remember being with a woman. She had so much verve and personality he couldn't take his eyes off her and the awareness that he was taking her home to bed gave him a supreme high of satisfaction.

A week later she dragged him out to the flower market on Columbia Road and he took a photograph of her, her slender figure almost lost in the giant armful of flowers he had bought her. They walked along the South Bank and he watched street performers entertain for the first time ever, laughing when she called him a stuffed shirt for admitting that.

'You can't always have been so sensible, so careful about everything you do and say,' she remarked with a frown.

'I learned to consider everything I did and said when I was very young,' Vitale confided. 'As a child, I was always trying to please my mother but eventually I gave up. I don't think she much likes children…or maybe it was only me.'

Jazz was shocked. 'You don't think she liked you even as a child?'

Vitale frowned. 'If being a queen hadn't demanded that she produce an heir I don't think she would ever have had children. I was a typical little boy—noisy, dirty and always asking inconvenient questions. She often cut short the time she was supposed to spend with me because I irritated her.'

'But you were only being a normal kid,' Jazz contended feelingly, catching his taut fingers in hers to squeeze them and gazing up at his shadowed features. 'That wasn't about you, it was about her and her flaws, not yours. Obviously she didn't enjoy being a mother but that wasn't your problem and you shouldn't let it make you feel guilty or responsible. You're an adult now and you don't need her the same way.'

That was certainly true, Vitale conceded, thinking back to his cold, distant relationship with his mother and his once childish efforts to improve it and win her approval. But as an adult he *knew* Sofia Castiglione now and he no longer expected her to change or tried to please her. Maturity had taught him that he was tough enough to get by on his own.

'I don't feel guilty,' he told Jazz, 'but I do get embarrassed when she treats people badly. When you're born into a privileged life like ours, you can't take it for granted and you can't afford to forget that you rule, not just by right of birth but only with the agreement and the support of the people.'

He was a deeper thinker than she had ever acknowledged and she was impressed by that distinction that he made. By the sound of it, his mother was a right old horror, she thought ruefully, annoyed that Vitale had clearly been so damaged by the wretched woman's inability to love her son. That night she lay awake for a long time, secure in the circle of Vitale's arms, thinking with warm appreciation of how tender he could be with her even though he had evidently had very little tenderness shown to him. He was so much more than he seemed on the outside…

'But I can't be… I'm flying to Italy tomorrow,' Jazz framed without comprehension because what she had been told had come as such a gigantic shock that every scrap of natural colour had drained from her rigid face.

'You're pregnant, around six weeks along,' the brisk female doctor repeated quietly.

'But I'm on the pill!' Jazz exclaimed shakily. 'How can I be pregnant?'

The doctor consulted her computer screen. 'I see you've been taking the mini pill for menstrual irregularity. Have you been careful to take it at the same time every day? It can be a little less effective as birth control than other methods. For contraceptive purposes, I would have recommended an implant.'

'The *same* time every day?' Jazz gasped in dismay.

'That information would've been in the instruction leaflet with the tablets.'

Jazz winced, acknowledging an own goal. 'I didn't read it.'

The doctor gave her a résumé of the various conditions that could make the birth-control pill less reliable and then added that nothing was one hundred per cent guaranteed to prevent pregnancy and that there was always a tiny proportion of women who still conceived regardless.

Jazz was in so much shock that she collided with someone as she left the surgery and spluttered an apology before she wandered aimlessly down the street into a café to sit with a cup of tea and contemplate her predicament. Vitale would go spare, that was all she could initially think. He might even think she had done it deliberately and had lied about being on the pill. Vitale was a naturally suspicious man when it came to women.

Other thoughts began to intrude. She was pregnant. She hadn't thought she could be when the nurse had asked for samples on her first visit to the surgery. No chance, she had cheerfully told the nurse, secure in her conviction that she could not conceive. But she had gone to the surgery in the first place because she was having troublesome symptoms. Very tender breasts, heartburn, occasional bouts of dizziness, increasing nausea and a sensitivity towards certain smells. Ironically she had suspected the pill, the only medication she took, might be causing those effects and had thought she might be offered another brand to try. Oh, dear heaven, what was she going to tell her mother? Her mother would be so disappointed in her daughter when she became a single parent…

Jazz heaved a distraught sigh, her eyes stinging madly. Peggy Dickens had always been very frank about the reality that *she* had had to get married back in the days in Ireland when a man was still expected to marry a pregnant girlfriend. She had admitted that she would never have married her daughter's father otherwise because she had already seen worrying evidence of his violent temper. Well, there would be no question of marriage to worry anyone, Jazz reflected limply. Vitale was highly unlikely to propose to a housekeeper's daughter, whom he had hired to fulfil a bet.

But Jazz also knew that she wanted her baby. Her baby, part of her *and* Vitale, which was an unexpectedly precious thought, she acknowledged. And it would be a royal baby too, she reflected, because Vitale *was* a prince. Although maybe her baby wouldn't be royal, she reasoned hesitantly, because their child would be born illegitimate. They were only involved in a casual sexual affair, she reminded herself with painful honesty, because on some level that truth made her feel ashamed, as though she secretly thought she had traded herself too cheaply. There was, after all, nothing solid or secure about their current intimacy. For the sake of the bet, Vitale had trotted her out to dinner several times and once to a West End showing of a new film. Only it still wasn't a *real* relationship, was it?

For six weeks, she had suppressed the wounding fear that she was merely a convenient sexual outlet for Vitale because she was living in the same house. The only time he didn't share her bed was when he was travelling on business or returning to Lerovia to appear at some royal function. Should she have kicked him out of bed?

A rueful smile tilted Jazz's generous mouth. Pride said one thing, her heart said another. She loved having Vitale in her bed and his uninhibited hunger for her delighted her. Was that why she had never once said no? He behaved as though he needed her and that made her feel special and important. Perhaps that fiery sexual in-

timacy wasn't very much to celebrate but it was
certainly more than she had ever hoped to have
with Vitale and it made her happy.

Now it seemed that she was paying the price
for that freewheeling happiness. She must have
conceived right at the beginning of their relationship, she reckoned heavily, to be already six
whole weeks along. What was she going to do if
he asked her to have a termination? She would
simply have to tell him that she was very sorry
but, while her pregnancy might be unplanned
and inconvenient, she still wanted her child. *His*
child too, she conceded wretchedly, digging out
her phone to text him.

We need to talk when you get back tonight.

Problem?

Don't try to second-guess me.

She knew that if she wasn't careful he would
dig and dig by text until he got it out of her, and
it really wasn't something she was prepared to
divulge remotely.

The phone pinged and kept on pinging with more texts. More questions for clarification, Vitale getting increasingly impatient and annoyed with her for her lack of response. Maybe she shouldn't have said anything at all, maybe that would have been more sensible. But Jazz had always suffered from the kind of almost painful honest streak that made immediate confession a necessity. She ignored her phone and stared down into her tea, feeling as if the world had crashed down on her shoulders because her discovery meant that she and Vitale were already over and done.

The end, she thought melodramatically because what little they had would not survive the fallout from a pregnancy that she already knew he didn't want.

'Leave your phone alone!' Sofia Castiglione, the Queen of Lerovia, snapped furiously at her son in the office of the royal palace. 'I want you to look at these profiles.'

Vitale resisted even glancing fleetingly down at

the women's photographs lined up on his mother's glass desk and the neatly typed background
info set beside each. Even a glance would encourage his mother's delusions and he refused
to be bullied by her. 'I've already made it clear
that I have no intention of getting married *any*
time in the near future. It's pointless to play this
game with me. It's not as though you want to step
down from the throne. It's not as though we are
in need of another generation in waiting,' he intoned drily.

'You are almost thirty years old!' his mother
practically spat at him. 'I married in my twen-
ties.'

'And think of how well that turned out,' her son
advised sardonically, recognising that his mother
appeared to dislike him even more now than she
had disliked him when he was a child and wondering if that was his fault.

As a little boy he had found her scorn and constant criticism profoundly distressing. He had
soon discovered that even when he excelled at
something he did not receive praise. For a long

time he had struggled to understand what it was about him that evidently made him so deeply un-lovable. Did he remind her of his father? Or was it simply that she would have resented any son or daughter waiting in the royal wings to become her heir? Or was Jazz right and was it simply that his mother disliked children?

'Don't you *dare* say that to me!' the older woman launched in a tone of pure venom, her heavily Botoxed and still-beautiful face straining with rage. 'I did my duty and produced an heir and I expect *you* to do your duty now as well!'

'No, possibly in another ten years, *not now*,' Vitale spelt out with emphatic finality and strode out of the room to continue texting Jazz, whose refusal to reply was seriously taxing his already shredded temper.

CHAPTER SIX

'I SAW IT at the airport,' Vitale lied, because for some reason Jazz was staring at the very expensive snow globe he had bought her as though it had risen up out of hell accompanied by the devil waving a pitchfork.

Jazz could feel silly tears flooding her eyes, knew it was probably another side effect of pregnancy and inwardly cringed. Why now? Why now, this evening of all evenings, did he have to do something really thoughtful and generous? It was the snow globe to top all other snow globes too, she acknowledged numbly, large, gilded and magnificent, full of little flying cupids, whose wings looked suspiciously diamond-studded and, when you shook it, it rained golden snow rather than white. It put her Santa globe to shame, lowering it to plastic bargain-basement level.

'It's really, really beautiful,' she told him chokily because it was, it was divine, but even if it had been hideous she would have said the same because she was so touched that he had bought her a personal gift. The globe, unlike the new wardrobe and the jewellery he had purchased and insisted she wear, had not been given to facilitate her leading role in a bet to be staged at a royal ball. All of that was fake, like the fake accent she had picked up from the elocution and the knowledge of how to curtsy to royalty that she had learned. She was to pretend to be something she was not for Vitale's benefit.

'What's the matter with you?' Vitale demanded with a raw edge to his dark, deep voice. 'And why did you send me that weird text?'

Jazz's legs turned all weak and she dropped down abruptly on the edge of a sofa in the big imposing drawing room where she never ever felt comfortable because it was stuffed with exceedingly grand furniture and seats as hard as nails. 'Something's happened, well, actually it happened weeks ago although I didn't know it then,' she muttered in a rush. 'You should sit down and take a very deep breath because you're going to be furious.'

'Only my mother makes me furious,' Vitale contended impatiently, studying her with keen assessing eyes, picking up on her pallor and the faint bluish shadows below her eyes. 'Are you ill?'

Jazz focused on him, poised there so straight and tall and gorgeous with his blue-black hair, arresting features and wonderful eyes, and she snatched in a very deep breath. 'Not ill... *pregnant*,' she told him with pained reluctance.

Vitale froze, engulfed in a sudden ice storm. He stared back at her, his eyes hardening and narrowing, and she watched him swallow back hasty words and seal his mouth firmly shut again.

'No, you can say what you like,' Jazz promised him ruefully. 'No offence will be taken. Neither of us were expecting this development and I know it's bad news as far as you're concerned.'

'*Very* bad news,' Vitale admitted in shock, paler than she had ever seen him below his naturally bronzed complexion. 'You said you were on birth control. Was that a lie?'

'No, it wasn't,' Jazz assured him. 'But for whatever reason, although I didn't miss taking a single pill, I've conceived and I'm about six weeks in.'

'And we've only been together around seven weeks!' Vitale thundered, cursing in Italian only half under his breath, his lean hands coiling with tension. 'Right, the first thing we will do is check this out in case it's a false alarm.'

'It's *not* a false alarm,' Jazz argued but Vitale had already stalked angrily to the far end of the room to use his phone, where she listened to him talking to someone in fast and fluent Italian.

All of a sudden even the sound of his voice was grating on her because, within the space of a second, everything had changed in his attitude to her. His voice was now ice-cool and his gaze had blanked her because he was determined to reveal no normal human reaction beyond that '*very* bad news', which really, when she thought about it, said all that she needed to hear and know. He had seemed so relaxed with her before and now that was gone, probably never to return.

Vitale studied Jazz while he spoke to his friend and discomfiture lanced through him. No, it wasn't a deliberate conception, and he knew that because he trusted her, and there she sat as if the roof had fallen in on top of her and she wasn't a skilled enough actress to look like that if that wasn't how she truly felt. Pregnant? *A baby?* Vitale was shattered but, unlike his brother Angel, he wouldn't make the mistake of running away from his responsibilities. He also knew that Jazz was a devout churchgoer from a rural Irish Catholic background and that a termination was a choice she was unlikely to make. He would be a father whether he liked it or not. But, before he agonised over that truth and its consequences, he was determined to take her to see a gynaecologist, who was a close friend and could be trusted to be discreet.

'Giulio Verratti is a close friend, whom I've known since my teens,' he volunteered stiffly. 'He also has a private practice as a consultant gynaecologist here in London.'

In silence, Jazz nodded, resigned to his need for a second opinion.

'I'll feel happier if he confirms it,' Vitale completed grimly.

Jazz thought that that was the wrong choice of words because the taut, forbidding lines of Vitale's lean, strong face suggested he might never be happy again. Regret filled her to overflowing. Her announcement had destroyed their affair. It would have ended anyway after the royal ball, she reminded herself ruefully. There had always been a clock ticking on their relationship and the ball was now only a week away.

'Let's talk about something else,' Vitale suggested as he steered her out to the waiting limo.

'How can we?' Jazz exclaimed.

'How do you feel about this situation?' he shot at her without warning.

'I was devastated at first,' Jazz confided. 'But now I can't help being a little bit excited too… Sorry.'

'You don't need to apologise,' Vitale intoned. 'Obviously you like children.'

'Don't you?'

'It's not something I've thought about. It's something I assumed was light years away in the future,' he breathed tautly.

He had defrosted a tad and she wanted to reach for his hand but resisted the temptation, recognising that it was not a good moment. Only two nights back, he had slept with her in his arms all night, but those days were over, she thought sadly. In a casual affair, a pregnancy was divisive, a source of concern rather than celebration. He would want their child to remain a secret as well, she mused unhappily. He wouldn't want the existence of an illegitimate kid splashed all over the media. Would he want to be involved in their child's life in any way? Or would he hope that giving her money would keep her quiet and persuade her to accept that he could not play *any* sort of active paternal role?

Giulio Verratti was a suave Italian in his thirties with prematurely greying hair. They didn't even have to sit down in the waiting room before a nurse swept them into the consulting room and the gynaecologist explained the tests that could be done on the spot. The nurse shepherded Jazz off to perform the tests before Jazz returned to the plush consulting room where the results were passed to Giulio.

'You're definitely pregnant,' he announced.

Vitale's shuttered expression betrayed nothing to her anxious glance.

'I'm a little concerned by a rather high reading in your hCG,' he confided and he went on to offer her a transvaginal ultrasound, which could be more accurate at an earlier stage than a normal scan.

Vitale flinched. 'No. We won't put her through that unless it is strictly necessary for her health.'

'Are there any twins in your family?' Mr Verratti asked smoothly.

'Several,' Jazz volunteered. 'My grandmother and some cousins.'

'There's a strong possibility that this could be a multiple pregnancy and I'll do an ordinary ultrasound now to see if I can pick up the heartbeat or heartbeats yet,' the older man informed them calmly and he called the nurse to help Jazz prepare for the scan.

Gel was rubbed on her abdomen and a handheld scanner was run over her. Eyes wide, she stared at the monitor and then she heard the very fast sound of the foetal heartbeat and Mr Verratti laughed with satisfaction. He pointed at the monitor to indicate two blurred areas that he said were her babies. 'You do indeed carry twins,' he assured her.

Twins? Vitale had never worked so hard at controlling his expression. *More* than one child? The bad news just got worse and worse, he conceded helplessly. But every cloud had a silver lining, he instructed himself grimly. There had to be a plus side to even this disaster, although he had yet to see it. He would gain the heir his mother was so keen for him to produce but to achieve that he would have to marry Jazz, an alliance that Queen Sofia, the supreme elitist, would never agree to. But then he was fortunate that he did not actually require his mother's consent to marry. She had always assumed that, somewhere in the Lerovian tomes of royal dynastic law, such a prohibition existed but Vitale knew for a fact that it didn't. He was free to marry whomever he liked even if, at that precise moment, he hadn't the slightest desire to get married to Jazz or any other woman.

And he blamed himself entirely for taking on that crazy competitive bet with his younger brother, Zac. What insanity had possessed him? Of all three of the brothers, Vitale was indisputably the sensible, steady one and yet look at the mess he was in now! Somehow, he had contrived to choreograph his own downfall by moving a young woman into his home, whom he couldn't keep his hands off, he thought with raw self-loathing and distaste. He had known from the outset that Jazz attracted him and he had still gone ahead, believing that he had vast self-discipline and learning differently very, very quickly.

And it was hardly surprising that it threatened to be a multiple pregnancy, he conceded even more grimly, considering that they had been having sex every night for weeks on end. Not once had he used a condom as an extra safeguard. His *own* mistakes, his own indefensible errors of judgement, piled up on top of Vitale like a multiple road crash and plunged him into brooding silence.

Jazz lay awake alone most of that night. Vitale had barely spoken after leaving Mr Verratti's surgery. He hadn't even come to say goodnight to her, indeed had been noticeably careful not to touch her again in any way. It was as if she now had a giant defensive forcefield wrapped round her. Or as if her sudden overwhelming attraction had just died the very instant he'd realised she was pregnant with twins. The truth of their predicament was finally settling in on him and of course, he was upset. But she had kind of—secretly—hoped he would come to her if he was upset, as he had one other night after a more than usually distressing argument on the phone with his shrewish mother. He had shared that with her and she had felt important to him in a different way for the first time.

A little less fanciful now, she sat up in bed and put on the light to study her gilded and very ornate snow globe and her eyes simply overflowed again, tears trickling down her cheeks while she sniffed and dashed them away and generally hated herself for being such a drip. She had got attached to him, hadn't she? She was *more than fond* of Vitale after so many weeks of living with him.

How had she felt as though they were tailor-made for each other when that was so patently untrue? She, a housekeeper's daughter, he, a royal prince? Would he even continue with the bet now? He wouldn't want her in the public eye again, she reckoned, wouldn't wish to be associated with a woman who would be looking very pregnant in a few months' time. When Mr Verratti had mentioned that provocative word, 'twins', Vitale had looked as though he had been hand sculpted out of granite. She had practically heard Vitale thinking that *one* child would have been quite enough to contend with. She recognised that she was getting all het up with no prospect of calming herself down again. Eventually sheer exhaustion made her sleep.

First thing the next morning, she found herself in the bathroom being horribly sick and that shift from nausea to actual illness felt like the last straw. Washing away the evidence, she examined her wan reflection in the mirror and decided she had a slight greenish cast that was not the tiniest bit attractive. The sore boobs squashed into a bra that had become too small didn't help either, she thought miserably as she got dressed, selecting jeans and a colourful top in the hope of looking brighter and less emotionally sensitive than she actually felt.

She walked slowly downstairs. Vitale appeared in the dining-room doorway.

'Breakfast… Join me,' he suggested in that same hatefully distant tone.

'I didn't want this development either,' she said in her own defence as she moved past him, avoiding looking at him quite deliberately.

'I think I know that,' he conceded curtly.

Her bright head flew up and she looked at him. *'Do you?'*

Exasperation flared in his forbidding gaze. 'Yes, but it doesn't change the situation.'

She supposed it didn't. He accepted that she wasn't guilty of intent but somehow she still felt that she was being held to blame. And possibly she *was* to blame, thinking about the instructions she had failed to read because at the time contraception had not been an issue she'd cared about or needed. She had assumed she was safe from conception when she wasn't but he had made the same assumption. What did it matter now anyway? He was right. A lack of intent didn't change anything.

She lifted a plate and helped herself to toast and butter, her unsettled stomach cringing at the prospect of anything more solid.

'Shouldn't you be having something more to eat?'

'I'm nauseous. That's why I went to the doctor in the first place,' she admitted stiltedly as Jenkins poured tea and coffee while Vitale simply ignored the older man's presence.

When the butler had closed the door on his exit, Vitale studied her and said flatly, 'We have to get married and quickly.'

Jazz stared back at him wide-eyed and stunned by incredulity at that declaration. 'That's ludicrous!' she gulped.

'No, it isn't. There is another dimension to this issue which you are ignoring but which I cannot ignore,' Vitale imparted coolly. 'The children you carry will be heirs to the throne of Lerovia with the firstborn taking precedence. If they are born illegitimate they *cannot* be heirs and I know that I don't want a child of mine in this world that feels cheated of their birthright because I failed to marry you.'

He was quite correct. Jazz had not considered that issue in any depth or how any such child would feel as he or she grew up and realised the future they had been denied by an accident of birth. She swallowed hard but still said, 'Be sensible, Vitale. You can't marry someone like me. You're a prince.'

'I don't think we have a choice. We'll get married very discreetly and quietly in a civil ceremony and keep the news to ourselves until after the ball,' Vitale informed her.

'You're still taking me to the ball?' she murmured in surprise.

'If you're going to be my wife, why wouldn't I take you?'

'But you don't *want* to marry me,' she pointed out shakily. 'And feeling like that it would be all wrong for both of us.'

Vitale dealt her a cool sardonic appraisal. 'We don't have to stay married for ever, Jazz. Only long enough to legitimise our children's birth.'

'Oh…' Jazz reddened fiercely, feeling foolish for not having recognised the obvious escape clause in his startling announcement that they should marry. He wasn't talking about a normal marriage, of course he wasn't. He was suggesting a temporary marriage for their children's sake followed by divorce, a relationship that would be, in its own way, as false as the role he had already prepared her to play at the ball as his partner.

'And there *is* a plus side for me,' Vitale continued smoothly. 'I get the heir my mother so badly wants me to have and there will be no pressure on me to marry a second time.'

Jazz had lost colour as the true ramifications of what he was proposing slowly sank in, but pride made her contrive an approximation of a smile. 'So, everybody gets what they want,' she completed tightly.

Everybody but me, she conceded painfully, forced to listen to how he wanted to marry her and then get rid of her again after profiting from her unintentional fertility. She was seeing the side of Vitale that she hated, that sharp-as-knives, cold, calculating streak that could power him in moments of crisis. And it chilled Jazz right down to the marrow bone.

Inside her chest her heart felt as though he had stuck an actual knife in it. Over the past weeks, she had become attached but *he had not*. For Vitale, she had been a means to an end, a convenient lover, not someone he valued in any more lasting way. Now he planned to make the best of a bad situation and marry her to legitimise the children she carried. That would benefit him and it would benefit their children as well. But there would be no benefit for Jazz in becoming Vitale's temporary wife. Continued exposure to Vitale's callous indifference would only open her up to a world of hurt. And what on earth would it be like for her to become a member of a *royal* family? Ordinary women like her didn't marry princes, she reflected with a sinking stomach. How the heck could she rise to the level of a royal?

But, seriously, what choice did she have? She didn't have the luxury of saying no to what was surely the most unromantic proposal of marriage that had ever been voiced by a man. How could she deny her unborn twins the right to become accepted members of the Lerovian royal family? That would be a very selfish thing to do, to protect herself instead of securing her children's future. And she could see that Vitale had not a doubt that she would accept his proposal, which made her want to throw a plate of really messy jelly at him. All those years being chased by princess-title-hunters hadn't done him any favours in the ego department. Evidently, he believed he was a hell of a catch, even on a temporary basis. Below her lowered lashes, her green eyes flared with slow-burning anger. He was rich and handsome and titled. He put in a terrific performance in bed and bought a good snow globe. But really, what else did he have to offer? Certainly not sensitivity, anyhow.

'We'll be married within a few days.'

Vitale dealt her an expectant appraisal as if he was hoping she would jump about with excitement or, at the very least, loose an unseemly whoop of appreciation. Cinderella got her Prince Charming—*not*, she recognised angrily. He hadn't even asked her if she wanted to marry him because he took assent for granted. And why not? The marriage wouldn't last any longer than possibly eighteen months and then he would be free again, free of the housekeeper's daughter and her baggage.

'My babies live with me,' Jazz declared combatively, lest he be cherishing any other sort of plan for their children. 'I raise my children.'

Vitale lifted and dropped a broad shoulder, the very picture of nonchalance. 'Of course. I believe you have an elocution lesson now.'

Jazz flushed in surprise. 'I'm to continue with those lessons?'

'Naturally. For a while at least you'll have public appearances to make in your role as my wife. Your pregnancy, though, will eventually make it easier to excuse you from such events,' he pointed out calmly.

'You really do have it *all* worked out.' Jazz rose stiffly from her seat and walked out of the room without a backward glance.

Vitale gritted his even white teeth in frustration. He would never understand women if he lived to be a thousand! What was wrong with her now? Why was she sulking? Jazz didn't sulk. She was never moody. He liked that about her. So, what was the problem?

During a long, sleepless night he had contrived

to find the silver lining in their predicament and he had been satisfied with the solution he had chosen. Why wasn't *she* delighted? He was willing to marry her, jump through all the hoops he had always avoided, just for her benefit and the twins'. OK, his wide sensual mouth curled, he wasn't saying that there wasn't *anything* in the arrangement for him. Jazz officially in his bed would be a personal gain, a sort of compensation for the pain and sacrifice of getting shackled at a mere twenty-eight years old to a woman his mother would despise and attack for her commonplace background. Anger flooded him. What more could he do in the circumstances?

On the morning of Jazz's wedding day, three days later, sunshine flooded into the apartment living area but she still didn't feel the slightest bit bridal. Sworn to secrecy, her mother and her aunt were attending the ceremony, but the very fact that Vitale had not asked to meet her family beforehand only emphasised to Jazz how fake their wedding would be. Angel and his wife, Merry, were to attend as witnesses.

In the preceding three days, Jazz had gone shopping for the first time armed with a credit card given to her by Vitale. She had got fitted for new bras and had picked an off-white dress and matching jacket to wear. But it had not been a happy time for Jazz. Her mother, Peggy, had been distraught when Jazz had announced that she had fallen pregnant by Vitale. It had taken her daughter and her sister's combined efforts to persuade the older woman that Jazz's pregnancy did not have to be viewed as a catastrophe when Vitale was about to marry her. Naturally Jazz had not even hinted to either woman that Vitale was not planning on a 'for ever' marriage.

That, for the moment, was her secret, her private business, she thought ruefully, but pretending for the sake of her mother and her family that Vitale genuinely cared enough about her to *want* to marry her cost her sleep. Her bouts of sickness had become worse and when, the second evening, Vitale had walked into her bedroom and found her being horribly ill in the bathroom he had insisted on asking his friend, Giulio, to make a house call. Mr Verratti had told her that the excessive sickness was probably the result of her twin pregnancy, warned her about the danger of dehydration and given her medication that would hopefully reduce the nausea. None of those experiences had lifted Jazz's low spirits or the horrible feeling of being trapped in a bad and challenging situation over which she had no control.

'How do you feel?' was Vitale's first question when they met at the register office, because Peggy Dickens had begged her daughter to spend that last night at home in her aunt's apartment, which had meant, traditional or otherwise, that Jazz had had very little sleep resting on a lumpy couch after having enjoyed the luxury of a bed of her own for weeks.

'I'm fine,' she lied politely, turning to greet Angel, who was smiling, and then be introduced to his glowing dark-haired wife, who was wonderfully warm and friendly. But Jazz went red, just knowing by the lingering look Angel gave her that he knew she was pregnant as well and she felt humiliated and exposed while wondering if Angel's wife was being so nice because she pitied her.

'I should have said that you look amazing in cream,' Vitale said hastily, as if belatedly grasping that that was more what people expected from a bridegroom than an enquiry about her health.

Not so amazing that he had felt any desire to so much as kiss her since her pregnancy announcement, Jazz reflected bitterly. But then Vitale, trained from childhood to say the right thing at the right time, couldn't always shake off his conditioning. In the future, she expected him to treat her with excessive politeness and distance, much as he had been treating her since she had told him she had conceived. And it hurt Jazz, it hurt much more even than she had thought it would to live with that forbidding new chill in his attitude towards her. It was as if Vitale were flying on automatic pilot and she was now a stranger because all intimacy between them had vanished.

If only she could so easily banish her responses, she thought unhappily, studying Vitale where he stood chatting with his brother and his wife. Vitale was a devastatingly handsome male distinguished by dark golden black-fringed eyes that sent heat spiralling through her pelvis, which made her avert her eyes from him uneasily. Her body still sang and tingled in his presence, all prickling awareness and sensual enthusiasm, and it mortified her, forced her to crave the indifference he seemed to have embraced with ease.

The wedding ceremony was short and not particularly sweet. For the sake of their audience, Jazz kept a determined smile on her lips and studied the plain platinum ring she had been fitted for only the morning before. She was also thinking about the very comprehensive prenup she had signed an hour after that ring fitting and her heart was still sinking on that score. That document had even contained access arrangements for their unborn children and a divorce settlement. Reading that through to the end had been an even more sobering experience. Vitale had thought of everything going into their temporary marriage and he had taken every possible precaution, so it was hardly surprising that any sense of being a bride escaped her.

'Give him time,' Angel urged her in an incomprehensible whispered aside before he departed with his wife, after a brief and extremely formal lunch at an exclusive hotel with her family. 'He's emotionally stunted.'

Vitale joined his bride in the limo that was taking them to the airport and their flight to Italy for a long weekend preceding the ball and said, 'It's completely weird seeing Angel like that with a woman.'

'Like what?' Jazz prompted.

'Besotted,' Vitale labelled with a grimace. 'Didn't you notice the way he kept on touching her and looking at her?'

'I noticed that they seemed very happy together.'

'They started out like us. Merry had Angel's daughter last year and at first Angel didn't want anything to do with either of them and now look at them,' Vitale invited in apparent disbelief.

'Already hoping for another child some day, he told me...'

Jazz perked up... Well, it was an encouraging story. 'Fancy that,' she remarked lightly.

'I wouldn't ever want to feel that way,' Vitale admitted.

'Why not?' she asked boldly.

The silence dragged and she thought she had got too personal and that he wasn't going to answer her.

But Vitale was grimacing. 'I saw my father crying once. I was very young but it made a big impression on me. He explained that he wouldn't be living with my mother and I any longer. They were splitting up. At the time, I didn't really understand that but later, when I looked back, I understood. I don't know why they divorced but I don't think it was related to anything Papa did. He was heartbroken.'

Jazz winced but persisted. 'Didn't you ask him why they broke up?'

'I never liked to. I was afraid of upsetting him. He's a very emotional man.'

But Jazz was thinking of Vitale as a little boy seeing his father distraught over the loss of a woman. Had that disturbing glimpse put Vitale off falling in love? After all, he already had a mother in his life who must surely have damaged his ability to trust women. Exposed to Charles's heartbreak, Vitale must always have tried to protect himself from getting too attached to a woman. After all, the very first woman he had been attached to, *his mother*, had rejected him.

'I should have invited Papa today and he'll be hurt that I left him out but I didn't want to get him involved in our predicament,' Vitale continued.

And that's the reward you get for digging where you shouldn't, Jazz told herself unhappily. Vitale knew their marriage would be a short-lived thing and that was why he had left his father out. 'Did you tell Angel the truth?' she asked, even though she felt that she already knew the answer to that question.

'*Sì*...' Vitale confirmed quietly. 'I have no secrets from Angel.'

'Apart from the bet,' she reminded him.

And disconcertingly, Vitale laughed at that reminder with genuine appreciation. 'I felt it was so juvenile to try and one up Zac that I was embarrassed. I don't know what got into me that day at my father's office. Or that day when you told Angel about the bet. I was in a very bad mood.'

In the days that followed that meeting with Angel at Vitale's house Jazz had come to suspect that Vitale had been angry because he had misinterpreted her friendly ease with his older brother as flirtation, forgetting that when they were kids Angel had been as much her playmate as he had been. She had thought, even *hoped* that Vitale was possessive of her attention and jealous. Now she knew better, she thought wryly.

Feeling like a wet weekend, she stepped onto her first private jet, stunned by the opulent interior and the spaciousness of the cabin.

'There's a bedroom you can rest in at the far end,' Vitale told her helpfully as he opened up his laptop, evidently intending to work.

'I might just do that,' she said tartly since it seemed to her that he was hoping to be left in peace.

She kicked off her shoes, and removed her jacket and lay down on the comfortable bed and slept like a log. Vitale remembered it was his wedding day when he was warned that the flight was about to land and he strode into the sleeping compartment to wake Jazz.

She looked so small and fragile lying there that he was taken aback because Jazz always seemed larger than life inside his head. Not since she got pregnant though, he reflected grimly. That had changed everything for them both as well as adversely affecting her health. Giulio had advised him to be very careful because a multiple pregnancy was both more dangerous and more likely to result in a miscarriage and one could not be too careful either with one's wife or with children, one of whom would be the next heir to a throne. Blasted pregnancy, Vitale thought bitterly, because he could see how wan and thin she was already. Her appetite was affected...her mood was affected. Nothing was the same any more and he missed her vivacity and spontaneity.

Jazz wakened with a start to find Vitale bent over her, his stunning dark golden eyes grim as tombstones. In haste, she edged back from him and sat up.

'We're about to land. You'll have to come back out,' he warned her.

'I must've been more tired than I appreciated,' she muttered apologetically while wondering if her absence had even registered with him.

CHAPTER SEVEN

ONE OF VITALE'S security team drove the four-wheel-drive up what Vitale assured her was the very last twisting, turning road because Jazz was carsick and they had to keep on stopping lest she throw up. It made her feel like an irritating young child and the politer Vitale was about the necessity, the more exasperated she suspected he was. So much for the honeymoon she had assured her family he was taking her on, even if events had conspired to ensure they only got to take a long weekend in Italy before the royal ball in Lerovia. It would be the honeymoon from hell, she decided wretchedly.

And then the car turned down a leaf-lined lane and way at the top of that lane lay the most beautiful house she had ever seen. Not as big as she had expected, not extravagant either. It was a sprawling two-storey farmhouse built in glorious ochre-coloured stone that was colouring into a deeper shade below the spectacular setting sun above. It was surrounded, not by a conventional garden, but by what looked very like a wild-flower meadow and the odd copse of leafy trees.

'It's gorgeous,' she said, speaking for almost the first time since she had left the plane about something other than an apologetic reference to the reality that she felt ill again.

Vitale sprang out of the car and opened the passenger door with a flashing smile that disconcerted her, his lean, darkly handsome features appreciative. 'I thought you mightn't like it,' he admitted. 'It's not luxurious like the town house or the palace. It's more of a getaway house.'

'It'll probably still be fancier than I'm used to,' Jazz pointed out, simply relieved that he was acting human again instead of frozen.

A light hand resting at her spine, Vitale walked her down the path and into a hall with a polished terracotta tiled floor. Jazz shifted away from him again to peer through open doors, registering that the furnishings were simple and plain, not a swag nor any gilding in sight, and she relaxed even more, smiling when Vitale called her back to introduce her to the little woman he called Agnella, who looked after the house. Jazz froze to the floor when Agnella curtsied to her as if she were royalty.

'Why did she do that?' she asked Vitale as they followed their driver and their luggage up the oak staircase.

'Because you're my wife and a princess even though I don't think you quite feel like one yet,' Vitale suggested. 'I'm afraid you'll have to curtsy to my mother every time you see her because she's a stickler for formal court etiquette. When I'm King, which is a very long way away in my future,' he admitted wryly, 'I will modernise and there will be a lot less bowing and scraping. Unfortunately, the Queen enjoys it too much.'

'Is that so?' Jazz encouraged, stunned by his sudden chattiness.

'Yes, the monarchy in Lerovia would never be described as one of the more casual bicycling royal families,' Vitale admitted with regret. 'Life at the palace is pretty much the same as it must have been a couple of hundred years ago.'

Jazz pulled a face. 'Can't say I'm looking forward to that. How on earth is your mother going to react to me?' she prompted anxiously.

'Very badly,' Vitale told her bluntly. 'I intend to break that news by degrees for your benefit. You'll be attending the ball as my fiancée.'

'Fiancée?' Jazz repeated in surprise. 'How… For *my* benefit?'

'My mother is likely to go off in an hysterical rant and she can be very abusive. I don't want to risk her throwing a major scene at the ball and I'm determined to protect you from embarrassment. I'll tell her after the ball that we are already married but not with you present. Be assured that, whatever happens, *I* will deal with the Queen.'

Merely inclining her head at that unsettling information about the kind of welcome she could expect from his royal mother, Jazz walked into a beautiful big bedroom with rafters high above, a stripped wooden floor and an ancient fireplace at the far end. In the centre a bed festooned in fresh white linen sat up against an exposed stone wall while a windowsill sported a glorious arrangement of white lilac blossoms. 'I really love this house. Can't you just imagine that fire lit in winter? You could add a couple of easy chairs there and use that chest by the wall as a coffee table.'

Vitale blinked in bewilderment, stealing a startled glance at her newly animated face. 'What a great idea,' he intoned, although he had never in all his life before thought about interior décor or furniture. 'We could go shopping for chairs.'

'Could we?' A little of her animation dwindling, Jazz wondered why she was rabbiting on as if he were truly her husband and the farmhouse their home and her colour heightened with embarrassment. 'I was just being silly and imaginative,' she completed, kicking off her shoes and settling down on the side of the low bed because she was tired, worn down by her stress and her worries.

'We'll look for chairs. I hired a designer to do the basics here and never added anything else,'

Vitale repeated a shade desperately, keen to keep the conversation afloat even if he had to talk about furniture to do it. He could not stand to see Jazz look so sad and her interest in the farmhouse had noticeably lifted her mood for the first time that day. Considering that it had been their wedding day, Vitale felt very much to blame. 'I didn't really have the time to think about finishing touches but I'm grateful for any advice.'

'I'm sure you could hire another interior designer,' Jazz told him quellingly, recalling the wealth of the male she was addressing and feeling even more foolish.

'I'd prefer you to do it,' Vitale asserted in growing frustration, having watched her face dim again as though a light had been switched out. 'You won't make it too grand.'

'Well, no,' Jazz agreed dulcetly. 'I have no experience of grand, so I could hardly make it that way.'

He watched her slight shoulders slump again and strode forward. 'Would you like to wear

your engagement ring?' he asked with stagger-
ing abruptness.

'My...*what*?'

Eager to employ any distraction available to
him, Vitale dug a ring box out of his pocket
and flipped it open, it being his experience that
women loved jewellery. Although, as he extended
the opulent emerald and diamond ring, he was
belatedly recalling that Jazz had been annoyingly
reluctant even to accept the basics like a gold
watch and plain gold stud earrings from him.

'Lovely,' Jazz said woodenly, making no move
to claim the ring.

Vitale's strong jawline squared with stubborn
determination. He lifted her limp hand and
threaded the diamond ring onto her finger until
it rested up against her wedding ring. 'What do
you think?' he was forced to prompt when the
silence stretched on even after she had snatched
her hand back.

'Stunning,' Jazz said obediently since she could
see it was expected of her.

'It is yours. I'm not going to ask for it back!'

Vitale launched down at her with sudden impatience, wondering if that was the problem. 'When we split up, everything I have given you is yours!'

Instead of being reassured, Jazz flinched and rose upright in a sudden movement, colour sparking over her cheekbones. 'And isn't that a lovely thing to say to me on our wedding day?' she condemned sharply. 'Of course, it wasn't a *real* wedding day, was it?'

Thoroughly taken aback by her angry, aggressive stance, Vitale stared at her with bemused dark eyes. 'It felt real enough to me.'

'But it *wasn't* real! Did you think I was in any danger of forgetting that for a moment? Well, don't worry yourself! I wasn't in danger of forgetting for a *single* moment. I had no wedding dress. You haven't touched me since I told you I was pregnant, not even to kiss the bride! I know it's all fake, like the stupid wedding ring and the ceremony and now an even stupider engagement ring. You don't *want* to be engaged or married to me. Did you think that little piece of reality could possibly have escaped my notice?' she demanded wrathfully at the top of her voice, which echoed loudly up into the rafters.

'I didn't want to be engaged or married to anyone,' Vitale confessed in a driven undertone while he tried to work out what they were arguing about. 'But if I have to be, you would definitely be my first choice.'

'Oh, that makes me feel *so* much better!' Jazz flung so sarcastically that even Vitale picked up on it.

Instantly Vitale regretted admitting that he hadn't wanted to be engaged or married to anyone. Was that quite true though? He had looked at Jazz throughout the day and had felt amazingly relaxed about their new relationship. But obviously, not kissing his bride had gone down as a big fail, but then Vitale had never liked doing anything of that nature in front of other people.

'I was trying to compliment you.'

'News flash…it didn't work!' Grabbing up a case from her collection of brand-new matching designer luggage, Jazz plonked it down on the bed.

'You're pregnant and you're not supposed to lift heavy things!' Vitale raked censoriously at her.

Jazz ignored him, ripping into the case, carelessly tossing out half the contents and finally extracting a robe. 'There'd better be a bath in there for me to soak in,' she muttered, stalking across the floor to the ajar door of the en suite, checking that there was and then recalling that she didn't have her toiletries.

In a furious temper she went back to check the luggage and, still finding the all-important bag missing, left the bedroom to go back downstairs and see if it had been left in the car.

Vitale released his breath in an explosive surge, genuinely at a loss. Somehow everything was going wrong. He had been too honest with her. He should never have mentioned splitting up or her keeping the jewellery. Angel had said women were sentimental and sensitive and all of a sudden that prenuptial agreement he had settled in front of her loomed like a major misjudgement. He had to turn things around but he hadn't a clue how and he sprang up again, concentrating on the overwhelming challenge of needing to please a woman for the first time in his life.

The bath, he thought, and then he had it, the awareness of her love of baths prompting him. He grabbed the flowers on the window sill up and strode into the bathroom like a man on a mission.

Hot, perspiring and cross as tacks after having to locate their driver and interrupt him at his evening meal to gain access to the bag that had been left in the car, Jazz made it back into the bedroom, which was comfortingly empty because she had had enough of Vitale for one day. She got to keep the jewellery, yippee, big wow there if she was a gold-digger but, sadly, she wasn't. She had wanted to keep *him*, not the jewellery, which was the sort of thought that tore Jazz apart inside and made her feel humiliated because Vitale had made it very clear that *he* did not want to keep *her*. She undressed and slid on the robe.

Entering the bathroom, Jazz was sharply disconcerted to find it transformed. The bath had already been run for her and candles had been lit round the bath, turning it into a soothing space while the lilac blossoms exuded a pale luminous glow in one corner. Rose petals floated on the surface of the water and she blinked in disconcertion at the inviting vision. Vitale? No, she decided. He wasn't capable of making that kind of romantic effort. She tested the water, found it warm and, with a shrug, she dropped the robe and climbed in.

Vitale pushed open the door, relieved she hadn't locked it, and extended a wine glass to her.

At the intrusion, Jazz jerked in surprise, water sloshing noisily around her slight body as she raised her knees automatically to conceal herself in a defensive pose. 'What are you doing?' she exclaimed, her voice sharp, accusing.

'Trying,' Vitale retorted curtly. 'Maybe I'm not very good at this.'

'*You* ran my bath, lit the candles?' Jazz gasped, wide-eyed with astonishment.

Vitale crouched down by the side of the bath, far too close for comfort, dark golden eyes enhanced by curling gold-tipped lashes stunningly intent on her flushed face. 'You're my wife. This is our wedding day. You're sick and you're un-happy. Isn't it believable that I would try to turn that around?'

Her soft pink mouth opened uncertainly and then closed again, her lashes fluttering up on dis-concerted green eyes. 'You don't usually make any effort,' she pointed out somewhat ungra-ciously.

'Situations change,' Vitale reasoned, speak-ing as though every word he spoke might have a punitive tax imposed on it and he were being forced to keep speech to the absolute minimum.

'I suppose they do,' Jazz muttered, accepting the glass. 'You know I can't drink this?'

'It's non-alcoholic,' he informed her.

Jazz sipped the delicious ice-cool drink and suddenly laughed with real amusement, startling herself almost as much as him. 'It's homemade lemonade!'

'My cousins visit me here occasionally. They have children and Agnella always likes to be pre-pared. She was my nurse when I was a child,' he confided. 'My mother sacked her when she reached a certain age because she prefers a youth-ful staff but Agnella wasn't ready to be put out to grass. She and her husband look after this place for me.'

'You're making your mother sound more and more like an evil villain,' Jazz whispered, for the bathroom with little flames sending shadows flickering on the stone walls was as disturbingly intimate as Vitale's proximity.

Vitale lifted and dropped a wide shoulder in si-lent dismissal. His jacket and tie had vanished but he hadn't unbuttoned his collar and, without even thinking about it, Jazz stretched out her hand and loosened the button, spreading the edges apart to show off his strong brown throat. 'There, now you look more relaxed,' she proclaimed, colour-ing a little at what she had done. 'Everything's changed, Vitale.'

'*Sì*...but we're in this *together*,' Vitale reminded her with gruff emphasis.

'Obviously,' she conceded. 'But I don't know where we go from here.'

'*We* don't have to change,' he argued with a

sudden vehemence that disconcerted her. 'We can go on exactly the way we were in London.'

'I don't think so,' Jazz declared, her heart quickening its beat with a kind of panic at how vulnerable that would make her, to continue as though she didn't know her happiness was on a strict timeline with a definite ending. She had to protect herself, be sensible and look to the future. Continuing what they had shared before now looked far too dangerous. 'I mean, since the moment I announced that I was pregnant, you backed off like I'd developed the bubonic plague.'

'Giulio warned to be careful with you.'

'Giulio? Mr Verratti?' she queried. 'He *told* you not to touch me? That we couldn't have sex?'

Vitale frowned. 'No, only to be *careful* and you were so obviously tired and unwell I respected the warning. Naturally, I left you alone,' he confided grittily. 'I didn't want to be selfish and I am naturally selfish and thoughtless. I was raised to always put myself first in relationships, so I have to look out more than most to avoid that kind of behaviour.'

He was so serious in the way in which he told her that that it touched Jazz. He knew his flaws, strove to keep them under control, didn't trust in his senses to read situations, never thought of explaining himself, simply strove to avoid the consequences of doing something wrong. It was a very rudimentary approach to a relationship and almost certain to result in misunderstandings. Jazz studied the disturbingly grave set of his lean, darkly handsome features and stroked her fingers down the side of his sombre face, fingertips brushing through a dark shadow of prickly black stubble.

'If you're coming to bed with me, you need a shave,' she told him softly, knowing she couldn't fight the way she felt at that moment, the yearning that was welling up from deep inside her to be with him again.

Right at this moment, Vitale was hers, and maybe she would never have more than a few fleeting moments feeling like that but did that mean she shouldn't have him at all? Yes, it would hurt when it ended but why shouldn't she be happy while she still could be? Wasn't trying to prepare for the end of their relationship now simply borrowing trouble?

Stark disconcertion had widened Vitale's dark gaze, letting her know that sex had not actually been his goal for once and Jazz smiled sunnily, replete with the feminine power of having surprised him.

'OK, *bellezza mia...*' His dark deep masculine drawl was slightly fractured and he vaulted back upright, sending her a flashing brilliant smile that made her tummy perform a somersault. 'I'll shave.'

And away he went to do it, where she had no idea, as she lay back in her candlelit bath, full of warm fuzzy feelings powered only by lemonade and candlelight. He had surprised her too and she was genuinely amazed by that reality. Vitale could be so very conservative and polite that it was often hard to catch a glimpse of what lay beneath. A man who was worried and concerned enough about their troubled relationship to run her a bath and put candles and flowers around it. Only a little thing though, much like her snow globe but it showed her the other side of Vitale, the side he worked so hard to hide and suppress, the sensitive, caring side. That could be enough for her, she told herself firmly, that could be enough to make the risk of loving him worthwhile even if it couldn't last for ever. Not everyone got a happy-ever-after.

He had said he was 'trying'. Well, she could try too, no shame in that, she told herself urgently, blowing out the candles and drying her over-heated skin with a fleecy towel before walking naked into the empty bedroom to climb into the bed and rejoice in the cool linen embrace of the sheets.

Vitale reappeared, closed the door and surveyed her where she lay, Titian ringlets spilling across the white pillows like a vibrant banner. Hunger leapt through him with a ferocity that still disturbed him. His motto was moderation in all things but there was nothing moderate or practical about his desire for Jazz. It was a need that took hold of him at odd times of the day even when she wasn't in front of him, a kind of craving that had creeped him out when he'd first learned that she was pregnant because what had been going on inside his head should, in his estimation, have killed all desire for her, not fuelled it. But now he didn't even have to think about that anomaly, he told himself with fierce satisfaction. They had reached an accord, he didn't know how and he didn't *need* to know, did he? How wasn't important; that the accord existed was enough for him.

'Jazz…' he breathed hoarsely, standing beside the side of the bed, wrenching at his shirt.

Jazz sat up abruptly. 'Come here,' she told him with a sigh. 'You just ripped a button off your shirt.'

And he dropped down on the edge of the bed and she unbuttoned the shirt, full pert little rose-tipped breasts shifting beneath his mesmerised gaze with every movement. He tossed the shirt, stood up, unzipped his pants, thrust it all down, ran irritably into shoes and socks while wondering how any male could be so impatient for one woman that he forgot how to undress.

Jazz spread herself back luxuriantly against the pillows.

'What are you smiling at?' Vitale enquired almost curtly, feverish colour scoring his high cheekbones.

'You look gorgeous,' she told him truthfully, admiring every long, lean, powerfully muscular line of his big body and most particularly the potent proof of his hunger for her.

Vitale could feel his face burn because no woman had ever said that to him before. He had never encouraged that kind of familiarity in the bedroom but that would not inhibit Jazz, who would say exactly what she felt like saying. There was something wonderfully liberating about that knowledge. He didn't know what it was, but it put to flight the stress of the long day and the very uncomfortable phone call he had just shared with his father.

'You *married* Jazz?' he had said. 'Your mother will throw a fit.'

But Vitale could not have cared less at that moment as he hauled Jazz up to meet his mouth, all
dominant male powered by seething hormones.
His hunger currented through her like a wake-
up call, setting every skin cell alight with his
passion. And Jazz revelled in that awareness of
his desire for her. It acted as a soother for other
slights and insecurities. Nobody had ever wanted
her the way Vitale seemed to want her. True, she
hadn't given any other man the chance, she conceded, but Vitale's passion made her feel ridiculously irresistible. His sensual mouth greedily
ravished hers, a knot of warmth already curling
at the heart of her in welcome.

And then his hands roved over her, those sure
skilled hands, fingertips plucking gently at her
swollen nipples, stirring an ache between her
slender thighs that dragged a moan from her because her whole body felt amazingly sensitised,
amazingly eager, over-the-top eager, she adjusted
in shame, squirming below his caresses, back
arching as he began to employ his carnal mouth

in a sweet tormenting trail down over her twisting length.

'Don't stop…' she exclaimed helplessly, her narrow hips writhing and rising until he caught them in firm hands and stilled her to withstand the onslaught of his sensual attention.

'Per l'amor di Dio,' Vitale groaned against her where she ached unbearably. 'If I had known I was this welcome, I'd never have kept my distance—'

'Pregnancy hormones,' Jazz cut in shakily. 'That's all it is.'

'Possibly multiple pregnancy hormones,' Vitale teased with unholy amusement dancing in his stunning eyes. 'Bring it on, *bellezza mia*. That aspect went unmentioned on the website I read.'

'Maybe it's just me,' she mumbled uncomfortably, her face hot as fire.

'No, it's intriguing to know a piece of me is in there,' Vitale growled, splaying his fingers across her stomach. 'It makes me feel like you really belong to me…weird,' he added for himself.

'All of it feels weird because it's wonderfully new to us,' Jazz reasoned, her fingers delving through his luxuriant black hair. 'I still can't quite believe it.'

Vitale let a fingertip trace lower and her head fell back, the power of speech stolen by an unexpectedly powerful flood of sensation that made her legs tremble. He bent his head and employed the tip of his tongue and her entire body jerked and shifted, little sounds of delight breaking from her throat that she couldn't hold back. And then there was no more talking because she was trapped in the relentless need for fulfilment, need controlling her, hunger roaring through her like a greedy tempest, craving more and crying out in wonder as he gave her more and the all-consuming clenching of her body powered her into an unstoppable climax.

'In bed, you're my every dream come true,' she whispered shakily, still rocked by the final waves of pleasure.

'It's the same for me,' Vitale admitted raggedly as he rose over her, forging a strong path into the tender flesh he had prepared to take him. 'It's never been this good for me.'

He plunged into her and withdrew in a time-less rhythm as old as the waves in the sea. Erotic excitement gripped her as she gripped him, lit-tle gasps racking her, tiny muscles convulsing around him. She quivered with sheer anticipa-tion as his pace quickened, stirring every atom of her being, driving her back up to the heights with every thrust until the bands low in her body began to tighten and she strained until he drove her over the edge again into glorious release. She watched him reach the same satisfaction as he shuddered over her, his lean, muscular body taut and damp and beautifully virile as he lifted him-self at the last possible moment, striving not to crush her with his weight.

'I feel good now,' Vitale husked, sliding off her and pausing to drop a kiss on her brow before moving away.

'I'm so pleased about that,' Jazz said laugh-ingly.

'You can hug me if you want. I've got used to it,' Vitale assured her arrogantly.

Jazz rolled her eyes at the ceiling. There he

was making allowances for her again but not actively joining in. She had taught him to tolerate being hugged but it wasn't enough for her. She needed *him* to grab *her* and hold her close and he wasn't going to do that. But at the same time she couldn't be a gift that kept on giving for ever. Shows of such affection from her would be thin on the ground from here on in, she told herself firmly.

'Are you in a mood?' Vitale asked quietly, leaning over her and gazing down at her with a very wary cast to his lean dark features.

'No.' Jazz stretched slowly and smiled. 'I'm hungry.'

'Agnella is holding dinner for us,' he volunteered.

'Holding it? You mean it's ready?' Jazz exclaimed in dismay. 'Why didn't you tell me?'

'It's fine. I told her you were in the bath,' Vitale explained with the carelessness of a male accustomed to staff who worked to his timetable rather than theirs.

'And how long ago was that?' Jazz groaned,

sliding hurriedly out of bed to head for the bathroom at speed. 'We should be more considerate,
Vitale.'

'It's our wedding night,' Vitale reminded her,
stepping into the spacious shower with her.
'That's different.'

'Don't you dare get my hair wet,' Jazz warned
him as he angled the rainforest spout. 'It takes
for ever to dry.'

Vitale laughed out loud and watched her wash
at speed and step back out again.

'You know there are other pastimes you can
enjoy in the shower,' he husked, humour sparkling in his dark eyes.

'We're going downstairs for dinner,' Jazz
told him squarely, leaving the bathroom to root
through the tangle of garments she had tossed
out of her case earlier and find fresh comfortable clothing.

Their evening meal was served on an outside
terrace shaded by vine-covered metal arches. A
silver candelabra illuminated the exquisitely set
table in a soft glow of light.

The first course arrived and Jazz tucked in with appetite, conscious of Vitale's scrutiny. 'What?' she finally queried in irritation.

'I like the fact that you enjoy food. So many women don't.'

'No, I think there's a certain belief out there that a healthy appetite in a woman is a sin and that it's somehow more feminine to pick daintily at food,' she told him, watching and copying what he did with his bread roll, still learning the little things she knew she needed to learn before she appeared at the fancy dinner that would precede the ball. Without warning, the concept of doing anything that could embarrass Vitale in public made Jazz cringe.

'You must have been appalled by my table manners when we were children,' she remarked uncomfortably.

'No. You were always dainty in your habits. But I will admit that I envied your freedom. You did as you liked and you said what you liked, just like Angel,' Vitale pointed out ruefully. 'I only ever had that luxury during those holidays. My childhood was in no way normal at the palace. My mother expected me to have the manners and outlook of an adult at a very early age.'

'I don't want our children growing up like that,' Jazz told him bluntly.

Vitale lounged back in his chair, all sleek, sophisticated male in the candlelight and devastatingly handsome. 'In that aim, we are in complete agreement,' he admitted. 'I want them to enjoy a normal happy childhood, free of the fear that they have to be perfect to be loved.'

'Does it matter to you whether they are boys or girls or even one of each?' she asked curiously.

'No. I have no preference. I will be very honest...' Vitale regarded Jazz with cautious dark golden eyes surrounded by gold-tipped lush black lashes. 'I have never wanted children but I have always accepted that I would have to have at least one for the sake of the throne. You have already achieved that requirement for me and to some extent, I can now relax, duty done...'

So, now I'm rent-a-womb, Jazz reflected, struggling not to react in too personal a way. He had told her the truth and she should respect that. *Duty done?* But he had *never* wanted children? That really worried her. His tender preparation of her bath had touched her heart and revitalised her but that blunt admission about never having wanted a child simply upset her again. All right, he was making the best of a bad job, as the saying went, but, as the woman playing a starring role and being made the best of, she felt humiliated and utterly insignificant in the grand scheme of Prince Vitale Castiglione's life…

CHAPTER EIGHT

JAZZ WAS UNPREPARED for the barrage of journalists and photographers who awaited their arrival at the airport in the capital city of Lerovia, Leburg. The amount of interest taken in her arrival with Vitale was phenomenal and she was no longer surprised by his request that she remove her wedding ring before their flight landed. Amidst the shouted madness of questions, flash photography and outright staring, Jazz felt as though she had briefly strayed into some mirror world, terrifyingly different from her own.

'The press know about the ball and my mother is too outspoken for there to be much doubt about its purpose, which was to find me a wife,' Vitale told her very drily when they had finally escaped into the peace of a limousine with tinted windows and a little Lerovian flag on the bonnet. 'So, obviously my arrival in Leburg with a woman is a source of great speculation.'

'But surely you've brought other women here?' Jazz exclaimed, still a little shaken up by her first encounter with the press en masse.

'You're the first. My affairs have always been kept off the radar and discreet,' Vitale explained reluctantly. 'Unlike Angel, I was never an international playboy and until today I have not been much troubled by the attentions of the paparazzi.'

'Did I hear someone shout a question about the engagement ring?'

'There were several, some in Italian and German,' Vitale advanced. 'That's why I gave it to you.'

'No, you gave it to me when you did because I was in a funk and you were trying to distract me,' Jazz told him wryly. 'Although I've no doubt you planned for me to arrive here flashing it.'

She liked the last word. His mother did as well. But somehow when Jazz cut in with one of her cute little last words, it didn't annoy him to the same degree, although her ability to read his motives unsettled him and made him feel tense. His lean, strong face clenched hard because he had already been tense. He hated conflict with Queen Sofia because it was a challenge to fight back when he was forced to give his aggressor the respect and obligation due to his monarch. It could never be a fair battle.

Jazz was merely relieved that she had put on an elegant dress and jacket for her arrival in Lerovia and had braided her hair, which left loose could look untidy. It had not escaped her attention that Vitale had grown steadily grimmer the closer they got to the country of his birth. Did he hate living in Lerovia, she wondered, or was it simply the problems he had dealing with his mother, the Queen?

She peered out at the city of Leburg, which appeared to have a skyline that could have rivalled Dubai's. It was an ultramodern, fully developed European city and a tax haven with very rich inhabitants, which she had learned from her own research on the internet. Furthermore, the man she had married, the father of her unborn twins, might be the heir to the Lerovian throne but he was also the CEO of the Bank of Lerovia. He hadn't told her any of that but then Vitale had never been much of a talker when it came to himself, so she wasn't the least offended by his omissions. In any case, she was perfectly capable of doing her own homework concerning the country where she was to live for the foreseeable future. Italian, German and English were widely spoken in Lerovia and many residents were from other countries.

The royal family had ruled Lerovia since the thirteenth century, which had disconcerted Jazz because for some reason she had always assumed that the Castiglione family were more recent arrivals. The ruling family, numbering only mother and son, lived in Ilrovia Castle, a white, much turreted and very picturesque building in the hills just outside the city.

Stealing a glance at Vitale's taut bronzed profile, she suddenly found herself reaching for his hand. 'You're not on your own in this,' she reminded him quietly. 'We got married for the sake of the children. I'm as much involved as you are.'

'No, you won't be. I won't put you in the path of my mother's spite. The Queen is my cross to bear,' he said very drily, quietly easing his fingers free. 'In any case, you're pregnant and you shouldn't be upset in *any* way.'

'Nonsense!' Jazz parried roundly, her backbone of steel stiffening but her pride and her heart hurt by the way he had instantly freed her hand. She gritted her teeth, inwardly urging herself to be patient and not to expect change overnight.

But even so, Vitale had been very different over their Italian weekend. He had been relaxed, not once retreating into the reserved and rather chilly impersonal approach that she was beginning to appreciate was the norm for him in public places or with strangers. Change had loomed only when they had landed in Lerovia, which really said it all, she thought ruefully. In her very bones, she was aware that she was soon to meet the mother-in-law from hell and that she had absolutely no defensive armour with which to fight back.

After all, she *was* the daughter of a humble housekeeper with no impressive ancestors, a little better educated than those ancestors but still without the official sanction of a degree even if she had almost completed one. And she was pregnant into the bargain, she conceded ruefully. She didn't qualify as an equal in Vitale's world. To put it bluntly, and Clodagh had, Jazz had married *up* in her aunt's parlance and Vitale had married *down*. Well, she was what she was and perfectly happy on her own account but it seemed only reasonable to expect the Queen of Lerovia to be severely disappointed in her son's choice of bride.

The car purred through a medieval stone archway guarded by soldiers, who presented arms in acknowledgement of Vitale's arrival. Jazz struggled not to feel intimidated as they entered a giant, splendidly furnished hall awash with gleaming crystal chandeliers and grand gilded furniture. Vitale immediately turned left to head up a staircase to one side.

'I have my private quarters in the castle. The Queen lives in the other wing and the ground houses the royal ceremonial apartments where official events are held and where we entertain,' Vitale told her on the stairs.

'You do realise that that is the only information you have ever given me about Lerovia?' Jazz remarked drily.

Vitale paused on the landing, dark golden eyes visibly disturbed by that observation.

'Oh, don't worry. The internet made up for your omission,' Jazz assured him ruefully. 'I've picked up the basics. It was interesting. I had no idea your family had been ruling here for so many generations or that gay people still live a restricted life here.'

He clenched his jaw. 'The Queen will countenance nothing that goes against church teaching. Unfortunately, the monarch in Lerovia also still has the right to veto laws proposed by parliament,' he admitted. 'I wasn't joking when I warned you that we lived in the past here.'

'Some day you'll be able to shake it up a little,' Jazz pointed out as he guided her through a door into a hallway that was surprisingly contemporary in contrast to the rather theatrical ground-floor décor.

'That day is a long way off,' Vitale intoned with firm conviction. 'The Queen will never voluntarily give up power.'

Jazz wandered round her new home, followed by two members of Vitale's domestic staff, Adelheid the housekeeper and Olivero, the butler. Both spoke excellent English and she learned that Vitale's wing had originally been the nursery wing devoted to his upbringing and in complete isolation from his mother's living accommodation. Obviously, the Queen was not the maternal type, Jazz acknowledged, knowing that she would never accept her children being housed at such a distance from her and solely tended to by staff. The more little glimpses she gained of Vitale's far from sunny childhood, the better she understood him.

Their spacious home stretched to three floors and steps led down from the big airy drawing room to the gardens. Jazz was smothering yawns by the time the official tour reached the master bedroom, which was decorated in subtle shades of green and grey. She was introduced to *her* maid, Carmela, who was already unpacking her luggage to fill the large, well-appointed dressing room off the bedroom. A maid, her own *maid*, she thought in awed disbelief.

Vitale entered after the maid had gone and found Jazz lying down on the bed with her shoes and jacket removed.

'I thought I'd go for a nap before I start getting ready for the ball. I'm really quite sleepy,' she confided, pushing herself up on her elbows, the braid she had undone to lie down now a tumbling mass of vibrant tresses falling over one shoulder, the arch of her spine pushing her breasts taut up against the fine silk bodice of her dress.

Vitale studied her with brutally male appreciation and a heat she was instantly aware of, his dark eyes scorching hot with the thought of possibilities, and something clenched low in her body, the stirring primal impulses of the same hunger.

'I'll leave you in peace,' he began.

'No,' Jazz countered, reaching out her hand to close into his sleeve. 'I'm not *that* tired.'

Vitale dealt her a sizzling smile that sent butterflies tumbling in her tummy and bent his head to kiss her, both his hands sinking into the torrent of her hair. Excitement leapt into her slender body like a lightning bolt and then just as suddenly the bedroom door burst noisily open. Vitale released her instantaneously and Jazz thrust herself up on her hands, her face flushed with annoyance and embarrassment as she focused on the woman who had stalked into their bedroom without so much as a warning knock. Even worse, a gaggle of goggle-eyed people were peering in from the corridor outside.

'Close the door, Vitale,' Jazz murmured flatly, staring at the enraged blonde, garbed in a stylish blue suit and pearls, standing mere feet away. 'We don't need an audience for this—'

'Oh, I think we do, leave the door wide, Vitale,' Queen Sofia cut in imperiously. 'I'd like an audience to see your red-headed whore being thrown out of the palace.'

Vitale closed the door and swung round. 'I will not tolerate so rude an intrusion, nor will I tolerate such abuse.'

'You will tolerate whatever I ask you to tolerate because I am your *Queen*!' the blonde proclaimed with freezing emphasis. 'I want this creature gone. I don't care how you do it but it *must* be done before the ball this evening.'

'If my fiancée leaves, I will accompany her,' Vitale parried.

'You wouldn't *dare*!' his mother screeched at him, transforming from ice to instant fiery fury.

A woman with no volume control, Jazz registered, only just resisting the urge to physically cover her ears. The Queen shot something at Vitale in outraged Italian and the battle commenced, only, frustratingly, Jazz had no idea what was being said. Vitale's mother seemed to be concentrating on trying to shout him down while Vitale himself spoke in a cool, clipped voice Jazz had never heard him employ before, his control absolute.

'Jazz will be my partner at the ball this evening,' Vitale declared in clarifying English. 'Nothing you can say or do will change that.'

'She's a servant's daughter… Oh, yes, I've found out all about you!' Queen Sofia shot triumphantly at Jazz, her piercing pale blue eyes venomous.

Jazz slid off the bed and stood up, instantly feeling stronger.

'You're a nothing, a nobody, and I don't know what my son's doing with you because he *should* know his duty better than anyone.'

'As you have often reminded me, my duty is to marry and produce a child,' Vitale interposed curtly. 'Jazz is the woman I have chosen.'

'I will not accept her and therefore she has to go!' The older woman cast the file she had tightly gripped in one hand down on the bed beside Jazz. 'Have a look at the candidates I selected. You couldn't compete with a single one of those women! You have no breeding and no education, none of the very special qualities required to match my son's status.'

'Get out,' Vitale breathed with chilling bite,

closing a firm hand to the older woman's arm to lead her back to the door. 'You have said what you came to say and I will not allow you to abuse Jazz.'

'If you bring her to the ball, I will not acknowledge her!' Queen Sofia threatened. 'And I will make your lives hell!'

'I imagine Vitale is quite used to you making his life hell,' Jazz opined dulcetly, her head held high as the older woman stared at her in disbelief, much as though a piece of furniture had moved forward and dared to address her. 'And as long as I have Vitale by my side, you will not intimidate me with your threats either.'

'Are you going to let this interloper speak to your Queen like that?' his mother raged.

In answer, Vitale strode forward and addressed his mother in an angry flood of English, a dark line of colour edging his hard cheekbones. The older woman tried to shout him down but Vitale slashed an authoritative silencing hand through the air and continued in the same splintering tone, 'You will not call my fiancée vile names *ever* again. You will not force your way into my private quarters again either. I am an adult, not a child you can bully and disrespect. Other people may tolerate such behaviour from you but I no longer will. Be careful, Mother, *very* careful because your future plans could easily fall apart. Your insolence is intolerable and if it continues I will leave the palace and I will leave Lerovia,' he completed harshly. 'I will not live anywhere where my fiancée is viciously abused.'

The Queen was pale and seemed to have shrunk in size. She opened her mouth but then just as suddenly closed it again, visibly shattered by his threat to leave the country. As she left, Vitale shut the door firmly again.

For an instant there was complete silence. Jazz was shaken by his vigorous defence but still unconvinced by his decision not to tell the whole truth immediately.

'You should have told your mother that the deed was already done and that you are married,' Jazz told him unhappily. 'Why wait to break that final bit of news when she's already in such a snit?'

'I have my own ways of dealing with my mother,' Vitale countered curtly. 'Don't interfere and give her another excuse to attack you.'

'There's more than one way of skinning a rabbit!' Jazz tossed back at him, determined to fight her corner as best she could. 'Could you have my cases brought back in?'

Vitale froze, a winged ebony brow lifting. 'Why would you want your cases?'

'Because if your mother is free to walk into our bedroom any time she likes, I'm not staying,' Jazz told him bluntly.

'*Dannazione...*' Vitale swore with clenched fists of frustration. 'You heard what I told her.'

'I just witnessed a grown woman throwing a tantrum and hurling outrageous insults with apparent impunity. Being royal, being a queen, does not excuse that kind of behaviour.'

Vitale ground his teeth together and raked long brown fingers through his cropped blue-black hair. 'I agree,' he conceded. 'But I threatened to leave this country if she interferes again and that shocked her.'

'Ask for my cases, Vitale,' Jazz urged, refusing to listen. 'We could have been *in* bed when your mother walked in and she wouldn't have cared.'

In a provocative move, Vitale settled his broad shoulders back against the door and braced his long powerful legs. 'You can't leave. I won't let you,' he told her lethally.

'If you can't protect me in your own home, I'm leaving.'

'Over my dead body,' Vitale murmured, dark eyes glittering with challenge even as he stood his ground. 'You *will* be protected. I will accept nothing less.'

In reality Jazz was more incensed by his stubborn refusal to take her advice. 'I still think you need to tell the Queen now that we are married, I'm pregnant and that the marriage is only a temporary measure,' she countered between stiff lips.

'You don't know what you're talking about!' Vitale could feel his temper suddenly taking a dangerous and inexplicable leap forward again.

Jazz angled her head back, aware of the flare of angry gold brightening his forceful gaze but quite unafraid of it. 'Well, of course I don't… You don't tell me anything. It's all too personal and private for you to share, so you hoard all your secrets up like a miser with treasure!' she condemned resentfully.

'Don't be ridiculous!' Vitale shot back at her quellingly.

But Jazz was in no mood to be quelled. 'You had no problems telling *me* that I would only be your wife until the twins are born, so I can't understand why you would be so obstinate about sharing that same information with your mother! After all, she'll undoubtedly be delighted to hear that I'm not here to stay.'

At that unsought reminder of the terms he himself had laid down, Vitale's lean, strong features set like a granite rock and the rage he was struggling to control surged even higher. 'Now you are making a most inappropriate joke of our situation, which I intensely dislike.'

Jazz's green eyes took on an emerald glow of rage at that icily angry assurance because if there was one thing that drove her mad, it was Vitale aiming that icy chill at her. She had been proud of him when he'd targeted his mother with that chill though. 'Oh, do you indeed? I intensely dislike a stranger blundering into what is supposed to be the marital bedroom when we're on the bed! She's the kind of royal who gives me Republican sympathies! I will never *ever* forget that woman calling me a whore and I won't forgive her for it either, no, not even if she apologises for it.'

'The Queen does not do apologies. You are safe from that possibility,' Vitale derided. 'Now, you will calm down and have lunch, which is being prepared.'

'You will not tell me to calm down!' Jazz raged back at him. 'I will shout if I feel like it.'

'You're pregnant. You need to keep calm,' Vitale proclaimed.

'That is not an excuse to shut me up!' Jazz hissed back at him.

Vitale startled her by striding forward without warning and lifting her off her feet to settle her down squarely on the bed she had only recently vacated. 'It is the only excuse I need. Lunch will wait until you have rested.'

'Do I look like I'm in the mood to rest?' Jazz argued fierily.

'No, but you know it's the sensible option and you have to think about *them*.' Vitale unsettled her even more by resting his hand with splayed fingers across her stomach. 'Neither of us want you to run the risk of a miscarriage by getting overexcited and pushing yourself too hard when you're already exhausted and stressed. The ball tonight will tire you even more,' he reminded her grimly.

Jazz had paled and she closed her eyes, striving for self-control, but she was still so mad at him and frustrated that it was an appalling struggle to hold back the vindictive words bubbling on her tongue. And then her green eyes flew wide again, crackling with angry defiance. 'Surely a miscarriage would *suit*—'

Vitale froze, wide sensual mouth setting hard, dark golden eyes flashing censorious reproach. 'Don't you *dare* say that to me!' he breathed in a raw undertone. 'They are my children too and I want them, no matter how inconvenient their timing may be! No matter how much trouble their conception may have caused us!'

Jazz had stilled, her anger snuffed out at source by the wrathful sincerity she saw in his gaze and heard in his voice. 'I thought you didn't want children,' she reminded him.

'I thought so too but for some reason I'm getting excited by the idea of them now,' Vitale admitted reluctantly.

Surprisingly, a kind of peace filtered in to drain away her anger. She was ashamed of what anger had provoked her into saying to him but soothed too by her first real proof that Vitale truly *did* want their unborn children, regardless of their situation. Given sufficient time, he too had adjusted his attitude and his outlook had softened, readying him for change. She closed her eyes again, drained by the early morning start to the day, the travel and all that had followed their arrival at the palace. Fit and healthy though she was, the exhaustion of early pregnancy was pushing her to her limits and the imminent prospect of the ball simply made her suppress a groan.

Vitale glowered down at her prone figure. She had lost her temper, lost control, he reasoned grimly, had barely known what she was saying. Wasn't that why he guarded his own temper? But during that scene with his mother one unmistakable reality had powered Vitale. His wife and his children *had* to come first because they depended on him. His mother, in comparison, was surrounded by supporters comprised of flattering subordinates and socially ambitious hangers-on, not to mention her chief lady-in-waiting, the Contessa Cinzia, who had never been known to contradict her royal mistress.

Jazz only stirred when a maid entered the room bringing a tray and she sat up with a start, blinking rapidly while wondering what was crackling beneath her hips. Her seeking hand drew out a file and a dim memory of the Queen tossing it there surfaced.

'Thank you,' she told the maid. 'I'll eat at the table.'

She settled the file down on the table by the window. Carmela informed her that her hair and make-up stylist would be arriving in half an hour and, killing the urge to roll her eyes at that information, Jazz lifted her knife and fork and then paused to open the file...

CHAPTER NINE

'BUT IF THIS belonged to your grandmother that means it's royal, so how can I wear it?' Jazz protested as she held the delicate diamond tiara that shone like a circlet of stars between her reverent fingers.

'You're my wife and my grandmother bestowed her jewellery on me in her will for my wife's use,' Vitale explained. 'And if that is still not sufficient reason for you, think of how it will enrage my mother to see you draped in her mother's fabulous diamond suite.'

Her green eyes glinted with amused appreciation of that sally and she sat down by the dressing table to allow Vitale to anchor the tiara in her thick hair. With careful hands, she donned the earrings and the necklace from the same box and forced a smile, refusing, absolutely refusing to think about what she had read in that ghastly file that very afternoon. She needed to be confident for the ball, was determined to look as though she belonged at such a glittering event purely for Vitale's sake. The prospect of doing anything socially wrong in his mother's radius literally made her stomach clench with sick horror.

'You look wonderful,' Vitale husked as she rose again, a slim silhouette sheathed in a green gown that glistened with thousands of beads. Cut high at the front, it bared her slender back, skimming down over her narrow hips to froth out in sparkling volume round her stiletto-clad feet.

'Wonderful enough to win your bet?'

Vitale, designer chic in a beautifully tailored evening jacket and narrow black trousers, groaned out loud. 'I couldn't care less about that bet now and you know it. Accepting that bet was a foolish impulse I now regret.'

Jazz smiled, the generous curve of her lush mouth enhanced by soft pink, and Vitale shifted forward, dark golden eyes flaring. 'No,' she said succinctly. 'If you knew how long it took the stylist to do my make-up, you wouldn't dare even *think* of kissing me.'

Vitale laughed, startling himself, it seemed, almost as much as he startled her, amusement lightening the forbidding tension that had still tautened his strong features. 'You're good for me,' he quipped.

But nowhere near as good in the royal wife stakes as Carlotta, Elena or Luciana or their equivalents would have been, a rebellious little voice remarked somewhere down deep inside her where the file had done the most damage by lowering her self-esteem and making her feel almost ashamed of her humble background. Shutting off that humiliating inner voice, Jazz drank in a deep steadying breath and informed him that she was ready to leave.

The female staff had assembled to see her ball gown and Jazz smiled, pleased by their approbation, secure in her belief that she had chosen well when she'd decided not to pick the plain and boring black dress that Vitale would have selected. With diamonds sparkling at her every step, she caught a glimpse of her reflection in a tall hall mirror and barely recognised that glitzy figure.

Vitale's arm at her back, they entered a vast reception room on the ground floor where pre-dinner drinks were being served. Glorious landscape paintings of Lerovia lined the walls. Waiters in white jackets served drinks below the diamond-bright light of the gleaming crystal chandeliers twinkling above them. Angel and Merry headed straight for them and relief washed through Jazz the minute she saw their familiar faces.

'Super, *super* dress,' Merry whispered warmly.

'And yours,' Jazz responded, admiring the elaborate embroidery that covered her sister-in-law's pale gown. 'Vitale didn't tell me you'd both be here.'

'Vitale's on another planet when the Queen Bee is around,' Angel remarked very drily. 'One thing you will learn about Charles's sons, Jazz. He didn't pick our mothers very well.'

'But Charles is so lovely that he makes up for that,' Merry chipped in soothingly into the rather awkward silence that had fallen, because Jazz would not risk uttering a single critical word about the Queen, lest she be overheard and embarrass Vitale.

'Yes,' Jazz agreed as Angel roamed off to speak to his brother.

Place cards were carelessly swapped at the dining table to ensure that they sat with Angel and Merry and Jazz tucked into the first course with appetite, striving not to look in the direction of the Queen at the top of the exceedingly long table.

'Why's Zac not here?' Jazz asked curiously. 'I was hoping to meet him.'

'He'll be at the ball. He's not a fan of formal dinners,' Angel explained. 'He hates restrictions of any kind.'

'Very different from Vitale then… Interesting,' Jazz mused, incredibly curious about the third brother and already conscious that although Vitale hadn't actually admitted it, he didn't seem to like his Brazilian sibling much.

An hour later, Jazz was busily identifying the

women in the ball room from their photographs in Queen Sofia's file, the 'suitable wives' file as she thought of it. And not a plain face or a redhead amongst the six candidates, all of them terrifyingly well-born, several titled, all possessed of the ability to speak more than one language, a high-flying education and a solid background of charitable good works. None of them would have required lessons on how to use cutlery or how to address an ambassador or curtsy to a reigning monarch. By the time she had finished perusing that damning file Jazz had felt horrendously inadequate. She had also felt ashamed that she had instinctively resented Vitale's certainty that theirs could only be a temporary marriage.

Of course, he didn't want to keep her when she was so ill-qualified for the position of a royal wife. Obviously, he would want a bride with all the accomplishments that he himself took for granted. Like with like worked best even in nature. It didn't mean that she was something lesser than the male she had married, she reasoned painfully, it only meant that they were too different.

'Zac's around here somewhere but I keep on missing him,' Vitale breathed impatiently, a lean bronzed hand settling to her slender spine as he walked out to the grand foyer where guests stood in clusters served by another army of waiters bearing drinks trays.

An older man intercepted them and urged Vitale to introduce him to his fiancée. 'Jazz.'

'Short for?'

'Jazmine,' she slotted in with a smile, because it was the first time she had been asked. 'My father registered my birth and he spelt it with a *z* rather than an *s*, which is how I became Jazz.'

'And a very good friend in the media told me that you've known each other since you were children,' the older man filled in with amusement. 'That's one in the eye for your mother,' he pronounced with satisfaction before passing on.

'Who was that?'

'My mother's younger half-brother, Prince Eduardo.'

'Your *uncle*?' Jazz repeated in surprise.

'My mother wouldn't even let him live here after she was crowned. She has always behaved as though she were an only child refusing to share the limelight...'

Jazz's attention had strayed to the male exiting from a room further down the hall, smoothing down his jacket, running careless fingers through his long black hair, his light eyes bright beneath the lights. 'Is that Zac?' she asked abruptly, recognising the resemblance.

Two giggling women, one blonde, one brunette in rather creased ball gowns emerged from the same room only one telling step in the man's wake.

'*Sì*...that's Zac,' Vitale confirmed with audible distaste. 'I wonder what he did with his partner while he was in there.'

A moment later, Zac answered that question for himself. 'Well, obviously you win. Jazz is amazing and I came alone,' he spelt out with a surprisingly charismatic grin of acknowledgement. 'My car is already in transit.'

While the brothers chatted, Jazz wandered off. Her mother-in-law was talking to a bunch of people at the far end of the hall and Jazz tactfully avoided that area.

Vitale rejoined her by sliding his arm round her back and she smiled. 'So, you won,' she commented.

'I set Zac up to fail. I feel a little guilty about doing that now,' Vitale confided in an undertone. 'But even so, this evening you have been a triumph of cool and control and I'm proud to be with you.'

Jazz gazed up at him in shock.

Vitale sighed. 'It needed to be said and I'm sorry that it took my kid brother to say it first,' he admitted.

'Who were those women Zac was with?'

'Willing ladies?' Vitale suggested.

'Don't be so judgemental!' Jazz urged. 'Nothing may have happened between them and Zac.'

'They're both on my mother's staff. I'm not in a charitable mood,' he admitted wryly. 'In any case, Zac is a player with the morals of an alley cat.'

Recognising that Vitale's judgemental streak ran to both sexes, Jazz almost laughed. She wondered if he had ever resented his inability to behave the same way. Of course, he had, she decided, of course he must have envied his brothers' freedom. Zac and Angel had freely chosen their lifestyles but birth had forced a rigid framework of dos and don'ts on Vitale and choice had had nothing to do with it.

'Did you ever just want to walk away from being royal?' Jazz asked him as he whirled her onto the dance floor for the opening dance beneath his mother's freezing gimlet gaze. But the ballroom was so colourful that Jazz was entranced as more and more couples joined them on the floor, the ladies clad in every colour of the rainbow, their dresses swirling gracefully around them, the men elegant in black or white dinner jackets.

'Frequently when I was a child, more often as an adult,' Vitale confided, surprising her with that frankness. 'But a sense of duty to our name must be stamped into my DNA. Although I consider the idea, I know I won't actually *do* it.'

And it finally dawned on her that the unhappiness she had sensed in Vitale even as a child had been genuine and that acknowledgement saddened her. Shortly after midnight, soon after the Queen's regal exit from the ball, Vitale accompanied her up to the door of their apartment and she knew he intended to go and tell the older woman that he was a married man.

'If you're going to confront your mother,' she had argued all the way up the winding staircase. 'I should come with you.'

'There's no reason for you to be subjected to hours of her ranting and raving. For a start, she will initially insist that my having married without her permission makes the ceremony illegal,' Vitale retorted crisply. 'I'm used to her hysterics and she won't even listen until she calms down. Don't wait up for me.'

Thinking about Vitale poised like a soldier, icily controlled in the face of his Queen's wrath, made Jazz's hands clench into angry fists of frustration. She had arrived in Lerovia with an open mind concerning Queen Sofia but that single scene in their bedroom had convinced her that Vitale's mother was a despotic monster. And she cared, of course she *cared*, she reflected as she got ready for bed and finally climbed into that bed alone.

She loved Vitale. Oh, she hadn't matched the word to the feelings before in an effort to protect herself from hurt, but the hurt would come whether she labelled her emotions or not. She loved the male who had lit her candles round her bath, who had held her close all night before they travelled to Lerovia. He was amazingly affectionate when he thought she was safely asleep, she conceded with tender amusement, but wary of demonstrating anything softer during the hours of daylight.

Angel had deemed his younger brother 'emotionally stunted', but he had been wrong in that assessment. Vitale bore all the hallmarks of someone damaged in childhood. He had taught himself to hide his emotions, had learned to suppress his pain and his anger to the extent that he barely knew what he felt any more. Yet he was working so hard at protecting her from his horrible mother, she thought fondly before she drifted off to sleep.

Breakfast was served to her in bed late the next morning and her phone already carried a text from Vitale, letting her know that he was attending a board meeting at the bank and would be out most of the day. She ate sparsely, awaiting the nausea that often took hold of her but evidently it was to be one of her good days and she could go for a shower and dress, feeling healthy and normal for once instead of simply pregnant.

Clad in an unpretentious white sundress, she went down the stone steps into the gardens to explore and enjoy the early summer sunshine. She was slightly unnerved to be closely followed by the housekeeper, Adelheid, and introduced to the very large plain-clothed man with her as her bodyguard. Striving to forget that she had company, Jazz went for a walk and then phoned her mum to catch up. She was sitting on a bench beside an ornamental stone fountain when a young woman approached her with a folded note on a silver salver.

'It is an invitation to lunch from the Queen, Your Highness,' the woman informed her with a bright smile.

Shock both at the form of address and the explanation of the note engulfed Jazz. Obviously, Vitale had spoken to his mother after the ball and the royal household were now aware that she was a wife rather than a fiancée. Even so, Jazz had expected the Queen to react with rage to the news that her son was married to his redheaded whore rather than a luncheon invite, and she was perplexed, lifting the note from the ludicrous salver and opening it while struggling to control her face.

Yes, she had also noted that the young woman delivering the note had been one of the women who had been in that room the night before with her brother-in-law, Zac. She concentrated, however, on the single sheet of notepaper and its gracious copperplate written summons and gave her consent to lunching with Vitale's mother even though she would much have preferred to say no. Vitale would probably want her to say no, but then Jazz was made of much tougher stuff than the man she had married seemed willing to appreciate. Sticks and stones would not break her bones, indeed they only made her stronger. In fact, if *she* could for once take a little heat off Vitale, Jazz was delighted to take the opportunity.

'My dear,' Queen Sofia purred, rising to greet Jazz as if she were a well-loved friend as soon as she entered the imposing dining room with a gleaming table that rejoiced in only two place settings set directly opposite each other. 'Vitale shared your *wonderful* news with me.'

And the wonderful news, Jazz learned in disbelief, was that she was pregnant with twins. The Queen also trotted out that old chestnut about the heir and a spare with a straight face. In fact, she seemed to be, at that point, an entirely different woman from the one Jazz had met so unforgettably the day before. Sadly, though, that impression was to be a transitory one.

'Of course, Vitale has left me to organise the royal wedding,' the older woman continued smoothly.

'Wedding?' Jazz echoed in astonishment.

'You may legally be married now but for the benefit of our country and the dignity of the family there must be a religious ceremony in which you are *seen* to get married,' Queen Sofia clarified. 'Didn't my son explain that to you?'

'No,' Jazz admitted, thoroughly intimidated by the prospect of a royal wedding.

'Of course, you probably think it is a great deal of fuss over nothing when you and Vitale will not be together very long,' the older woman continued in a measured tone of false regret that told Jazz all she needed to know about why she was currently receiving a welcome. 'But our people expect a wedding and a public holiday in which to celebrate the longevity of the Castiglione family's rule.'

Jazz was holding her breath after that stabbing little reminder that as a wife she would not be enjoying family longevity. 'Of course,' she said flatly, because clearly her private wants and wishes were not to be considered in the balance of royal necessities.

'We are so fortunate that Vitale married you quickly and that your condition is not obvious yet,' the Queen carolled in cheerful addition.

My goodness, the prospect of a couple of babies truly transformed Vitale's mother, Jazz thought limply.

'Obviously we will announce that a civil ceremony took place in London some weeks ago,' the older woman assured her. 'Not that I think these days people will be counting the months of your pregnancy, but it will add to what my PR team regard as the romantic nature of this whole affair.'

'Romantic?' Jazz exclaimed, wondering if she would ever work up the nerve to say more than one word back to the Queen.

The Queen waved a dismissive hand. 'Your low birth. Your having known my son from childhood. His apparent decision to marry out of his class,' she pronounced with unconcealed distaste. 'We know that is not the true story. *We* know he *had* to marry you but our people will prefer the romantic version—the totally ridiculous idea that he could have fallen madly in love with you!'

Jazz was now pale as death with perspiration beading her short upper lip. She could no more have touched the plate of food in front of her than she could have spread wings and flown out of the window to escape the spite of the woman opposite her. She swallowed hard on her rising nausea, determined not to show weakness or vulnerability. She pushed her food around the plate while the Queen chattered about how very quickly the wedding could be staged and about how she would have Jazz's measurements taken immediately for her dress. After the meal, she was shown into another room where a dressmaker did exactly that and then she escaped back up to the apartment feeling as battered and bruised as though she had gone ten rounds with a champion boxer.

Jazz now understood exactly why the Queen

240 CASTIGLIONE'S PREGNANT PRINCESS

of Lerovia was willing to make her the reluctant star of a royal wedding. The twins would be Vitale's heirs and that was seemingly important enough to the Castiglione dynasty to counteract his bride's notoriously humble beginnings. Jazz tried to comprehend her mother-in-law's unreservedly *practical* viewpoint. Vitale could have married a woman who did not conceive or a woman who had other difficulties in that field. Instead his heir and a spare were already on the way. The Queen despised her lowborn daughter-in-law but would tolerate her because Jazz was not in Lerovia to stay. Evidently, Vitale had told his mother the whole truth about his marriage and Jazz could not work out why she felt so wounded and betrayed by that reality when she had urged him to do exactly that.

There were no more secrets now and it was better that way, she told herself over a lonely dinner. The Queen would throw no more tantrums and would play along for the sake of appearances until Vitale and Jazz broke up. Everyone could now relax—everyone could be happy.

* * *

'You're having a bad dream… Wake up!' Vitale shook her shoulder.

In the darkness, Jazz blinked rapidly, extracted from a nightmare in which she was fleeing from some menace in a haunted castle remarkably similar to Vitale's home. 'I'm fine,' she whispered shakily. 'When did you get back?'

'Midnight.' His lean, powerful body perfectly aligned to hers. 'I let you down by not being here. I didn't expect my mother to invite you for lunch. I *told* her to stay out of my life. What the hell is she playing at?' he demanded in furious frustration.

'She's crowing about the twins.' Jazz sighed, drowsily stretching back into the reassuring heat of him. 'And organising a royal wedding.'

'You should never have joined her for lunch,' Vitale declared rawly. 'You should've said you were ill and left me to deal with her.'

'I managed. It was OK,' Jazz lied.

'I don't believe you,' Vitale admitted, flipping her over onto her back and leaning over her, his lean, darkly beautiful face shadowed by moon-light into intriguing hard edges and hollows. 'She would've been poisonous. Don't treat me like I'm stupid!'

'For goodness' sake...' Jazz faltered as he stretched over and switched on the light to stare down at her accusingly. 'She was a bit bitchy, little jibes...you know...'

'Of course I know,' Vitale asserted grimly, his strong jaw clenching hard. 'I've seen her in action many times when she wants to punish those who have crossed her. What did she say to you?'

'Nothing that wasn't the truth,' Jazz dismissed. 'That you *had* to marry me. Well, can't argue with that.'

Vitale swore long and low in Italian. 'Don't you understand that that is why I want you to stay away from her at all costs? I refuse to have you exposed to her malice.'

'It really doesn't matter to me,' Jazz fibbed with pride. 'It's not as if I'm going to be living here under her roof for ever, so I don't care what she thinks of me or what she says to me.'

'I care,' Vitale ground out fiercely, thinking of

what he had learned about himself after he had forced out the admission to his mother that his marriage was not to be of the permanent variety. 'I care a great deal.'

'Why are you in such a mood?' Jazz asked, running a teasing pale hand down over his bare bronzed chest, feeling him tense against her, watching his eyes flare with luminous revealing gold.

'I'm convinced you're a witch, *moglie mia*,' Vitale growled, his passionate mouth crashing down hungrily on hers.

Smiling inside herself, Jazz slid like a temptress along the long, taut and fully aroused length of him and, returning that kiss with equal heat, concluded the awkward conversation.

Three weeks later, Queen Sofia had the last laugh, after all, Jazz conceded as she watched her six bridesmaids fuss over her train and her veil, both of which demanded considerable attention due to their length and ornate decoration. Less was not more in the Queen's parlance, but Jazz had picked her favourite of the options presented to her. The pressure of starring as the leading light in a royal wedding sat heavily on her shoulders and it was several days since she had enjoyed a decent night of sleep.

It was a fairy-tale wedding gown and very sophisticated. It was composed of tulle and glitter net with a strapless dropped-waist bodice adorned with metallic embroidered lace. The neckline and waistline were richly beaded with pearls, crystals and rhinestones. Exquisite and stylish, the draped full skirt glittered with delicately beaded lace appliques. The veil was full length and fashioned of intricate handmade lace.

The bridesmaids, however, were a cruel plunge of a knife into Jazz's still beating heart. The file of bridal candidates she had hidden in the bottom of her lingerie drawer were all fully present and correct in the bridesmaids. So, naturally, Jazz was studying them, listening to their chatter, struggling to work out which one Vitale would eventually marry for *real*. Would it be Elena, who never ever shut up? Carlotta, who out of envy could barely bring herself to look at Jazz? Or Luciana, who either didn't speak any English or who didn't want to be forced to speak to the bride? Or one of the other three young women, all bright and beautiful and perfect?

The organ music in the cathedral swelled and Jazz walked down the aisle on the arm of Vitale's uncle, Prince Eduardo. Her family were present but her mother had shrunk from such public exposure when her daughter had asked her to walk her down the aisle, so the Queen had, once again, got her wish and had co-opted her brother into the role of giving away the bride.

Jazz was troubled by having to go through a religious service when her marriage was already destined to end in divorce but nobody had asked Jazz how she felt about taking such vows in church and she suspected that nobody would be the least interested in her moral objections. There was no fakery in *her* heart, nothing false about *her* feelings, she reminded herself resolutely as she knelt down before the Cardinal in his imposing scarlet robes.

Disconcertingly, Vitale chose that same moment to cover her hand with his and she turned her head to look at his lean, darkly handsome face, her heart jumping behind her breastbone, her tummy fluttering with butterflies while she marvelled at the compelling power of that sidewise glance of his and the curling lashes darker and more lush than her own false ones. His wide sensual mouth curled into a faint smile and she thought, Why is he smiling? and only then did she remember that there were cameras on them both and quite deliberately Jazz beamed back at him, doing what was expected of her, fearful of the misery inside her showing on the outside and equally fearful of doing the wrong thing.

Once again a wedding ring slid onto her finger and once again there was no kissing of the bride, Vitale being no fan of public demonstrations of affection. They left the cathedral to a barrage of whirring, clicking cameras and the roar of the irritatingly happy crowds assembled behind the crash barriers in the square beyond. It was lovely that people were happy for them, Jazz reflected, trying to find something positive in the event, but sad that those same people would be disappointed when their marriage ended again.

She would not miss being royal, she told herself as they stepped into the waiting horse-drawn carriage and Vitale complained bitterly about how rocky and uncomfortable it was to travel in such a way. Then without any warning whatsoever he gripped her hand, almost crushing her poor fingers, and shot something at her in driven Italian. '*Cosa c'e di sbagliato?* What's wrong?'

'Nothing's wrong!' she snapped, trailing her hand back in a trice.

'That is so patently a lie that my teeth are gritting,' Vitale told her roundly.

Well, that was tough but he would just have to live with it. She had been forced into a second very public wedding with the future replacement-wife candidates trailing her down the aisle as bridesmaids. Hadn't he even recognised them? Of course, he would have looked at the ladies in that file at some stage because his mother was too pushy to have let him sidestep it. Jazz felt very married and very cross with her two wedding rings and her husband who didn't love her. Not that that meant that he kept his hands off her though, she reflected hotly. Of course, she was in a bad mood. Yes, she was doing this for her children, but deciding to do it had been considerably easier than actually living the experience.

Vitale flipped mentally through every possible sin or omission he could have committed and acknowledged that he had made more mistakes than he could count. It made him uncomfortable when Jazz went quiet because she was never naturally quiet. 'Did the doctor say something that worried you?' he asked.

'Will you stop *reminding* me that I'm pregnant?' Jazz launched at him. 'Can't I just forget about being an incubator in a wedding gown for five minutes?'

Vitale clamped his mouth firmly shut because even he could take a hint that landed with the crushing weight of a boot. Maybe it was hormones, something like that, he reasoned uneasily. Or maybe she was feeling sick again. He parted his lips to enquire and then breathed in deep to restrain the urge, relieved that the palace was already in view. *An incubator in a wedding gown?* Where had that bizarre image come from? He would have a word with his father at the reception. Charles Russell had impregnated three women. He had to know something about pregnancy. Jazz sounded really upset and she didn't get upset, at least not in his experience. He stole a covert glance at her rigid profile and watched in absolute horror as a tear slid down her cheek.

'Jazz…?' Vitale stroked a soothing forefinger down over her tightly clenched hands. 'What can I do?'

'I just wish…' she began in a wobbly voice, 'that we were already divorced. Then it would all be done and dusted and in the past and I could get *my* life back.'

Vitale froze, his shrewd banker's mind going utterly blank at that aspiration. 'I don't want to discuss that,' he finally replied flatly. 'I don't want to discuss that at all.'

'Tough,' Jazz pronounced grittily.

Vitale decided at that point that talking was sometimes a vastly overrated pursuit, particularly when it was heading towards what promised to be a multiple-car crash of a conclusion. It was definitely the wrong moment. In a few minutes, they would be the centre of attention again at a reception attended by the crowned heads of Europe. What he said to Jazz needed to be said in private. It would have to be measured, calm and sincere even though it wouldn't be what she wanted to hear, even though he would be breaking his word. That acknowledgement silenced Vitale because he was appalled at that truth.

The reception was endless. Jazz shook hands and smiled and posed for photos, feeling like a professional greeter at a very upmarket restaurant. Charles Russell warmed her by giving her a hug and saying, 'Well, when I sent Vitale in your direction I wasn't expecting a wedding but I'm delighted for you both, Jazz.'

The older man greeted her mother with equal friendliness while Vitale bored the hind legs off her aunt by telling her all about Lerovia. At least he was *trying*, she conceded, striving to be more generous in her outlook. But that she was in a bad mood was really all his fault. They had supposedly only married to give the twins legitimacy, so why was he still sharing a bed with her? Why was he draping her in his grandmother's fabulous jewellery? She had more diamonds than she knew what to do with and he kept on buying gifts for her as well.

She thought about the tiger pendant with the emerald eyes that she cherished. She thought about the ever-expanding snow globe collection she now possessed. Vitale had given her the wrong signals from the outset and it was hardly surprising that she had fallen for him hard or that she had foolishly continued having sex with him, hoping to ignite emotions that he wasn't capable of feeling. He had as much emotion as a granite pillar! Didn't she have any pride or sense of self-preservation? Lashing herself with such thoughts, Jazz held her head high and continued to smile while deciding that things were about to change…

CHAPTER TEN

'THE STORY'S ALL over the internet...' a vaguely familiar voice was saying urgently. 'And apparently the *Herald* is publishing the article tomorrow, complete with revealing photos. Your mother's request that they pull the article was refused. The whole household is in uproar and Sofia's planning to flee to her Alpine chalet. Nobody knows how to handle this.'

'Yet you *knew* and you didn't warn me,' Vitale framed with raw-edged bitterness as Jazz peered drowsily at the clock by the bed and noted that it was three in the morning.

'It wasn't any of my business. She threw me out of the palace the day before her coronation. Saw her kid brother as competition, you see, refused to accept me as family.'

'*Sì*, Eduardo,' Vitale agreed flatly. 'I'll get dressed and see what I can do.'

'There's nothing anyone can do!' Vitale's uncle proclaimed on a telling note of barely concealed satisfaction. 'Too late for any emergency cover-ups now!'

As the bedroom door closed Jazz sat up and stared in the dim light of the lamp by the door at Vitale, naked but for a pair of black boxers. He looked shattered. 'What's happened?' she asked straight away.

'Apparently my mother's been involved in an affair with her best friend, Countess Cinzia, for over thirty years and it's about to be exposed in the press. The scandal's already online,' he revealed with harsh clarity.

'A gay affair?' Jazz questioned in astonishment.

'How did I *not* know?' Vitale groaned. 'That's why my parents divorced. Apparently, my father once found my mother and Cinzia together. After I was wakened and told, I phoned Papa at his hotel because, at first… I couldn't believe it. But he confirmed that it was the truth. Yet I *still* can't believe it,' he admitted with growing anger. 'I've lost good friends, friends who left this country because of the restrictive laws that the Queen actively promoted. How could my mother oppose gay liberation when she's gay herself? What kind of hypocrite behaves like that?'

'I don't know...' It was completely inadequate but Jazz could think of nothing to say because she was equally stunned by what he was telling her.

'I'll deal with it as best I can,' Vitale said angrily. 'But we won't be helped by the number of enemies the Queen's made of influential people.'

'Is there anything I can do to help?' Jazz enquired weakly.

'Go back to sleep,' Vitale advised succinctly. 'My mother will step down from the throne. She's too proud to face this out.'

'But *that* means...' Jazz gasped and then dismay sentenced her to a silent stare of consternation at the lean, powerful male poised at the foot of the bed.

'*Sì*. Let's hope you take to being a queen better

than you took to being a bride a second time,' Vitale pronounced with lashings of sarcasm while secretly wondering how he would take to the transformation of his own life. He could barely imagine a future empty of his mother's constant demands and complaints, but the prospect loomed ahead of him with a sudden brightness that disconcerted him, like the light at the end of a dark tunnel.

Jazz hunched back under the covers, too exhausted to snark back at him. She had collapsed into bed late the previous evening so exhausted that she had had all the animation of a corpse and had immediately fallen asleep. Certainly, it could not have been the second wedding night of any bridegroom's dreams. She had, however, been looking forward to escaping the palace in the morning and relaxing on the yacht Angel was loaning them for a Mediterranean cruise. Now she reckoned that any chance of a honeymoon was gone because, whatever Sofia Castiglione chose to do next, Vitale would be heavily involved in the clean-up operation and far too busy to leave the palace.

Vitale reappeared while she was having breakfast out on the terrace that overlooked the gardens. He told her that people were marching with placards outside the palace and that she was fortunate to be at the back of the building.

'How's your mother?' she asked awkwardly.

'She's already gone,' he breathed almost dazedly, as if he could not quite accept that astonishing reality. 'Cinzia and her together. She wasn't willing to talk to me and she released a statement declaring that her private life was exactly that, so no apologies either for a lifelong deception.'

'Did you really expect any?' She studied him worriedly, recognising the lines of strain and fatigue etched in his lean, strong face, and he shook his head in grim acknowledgement of that point.

The silence stretched while a member of staff brought fresh coffee to the table. Even the staff were creeping about very quietly as though there had been a bereavement rather than a massive scandal that had blown the Lerovian royal family wide open to the kind of international speculation it had never had to endure before. Jazz poured coffee for Vitale and urged him to eat. After his mother's hasty departure, he was heading straight into a meeting with government representatives.

'The Prime Minister persuaded her to abdicate,' Vitale groaned. 'Nothing to do with her being gay. Ironically, she could have come out of the closet years ago had she been willing, but she wasn't. It was her hypocrisy in opposing equality laws that are normal in the rest of Europe that brought her down. Her behaviour was indefensible.'

'Just move on from it,' Jazz muttered, feeling useless and helpless when she wanted to be the exact opposite for his sake.

'We all will,' Vitale declared more smoothly. 'But, more importantly, I've made arrangements for you, your mother and aunt to fly out to Angel's yacht this morning.'

'I can't leave you here alone!' Jazz exclaimed.

'There's nothing you can do here,' Vitale

pointed out with inescapable practicality. 'We have protestors outside the palace and in the city. Lerovia is in uproar. I cannot leave right now but you and your family can.'

'But—'

'It *would* be a comfort to me to know that you are safe on Angel's yacht and protected from anything that could distress you,' Vitale incised in his chilly take-no-prisoners command voice that always made her tummy sink like a stone.

Jazz's protests died there. He didn't want her to stay. He was sending her away. It was clear that her presence was neither a consolation, nor a necessity. It was a lesson, she conceded painfully, a rather hard lesson and overdue. Vitale didn't *need* her. She might feel a need for him pretty much round the clock but that bond did not stretch both ways. She sucked in a steadying breath and contrived a smile when she felt more like crying, a reaction he certainly did not deserve. 'OK. What time do I leave?' she asked quietly without a flicker of reaction.

Relief at her assent showed openly in Vitale's

stunning dark golden eyes and her heart clenched that her leaving could so obviously be a source of respite for him. Of course, he wasn't in love with her and he didn't depend on her, so she was, very probably, just one more person in his already very crowded life to worry about.

It was way past time she began accepting the limits of their relationship, she reflected unhappily, because here she was even now, always looking for more from Vitale, asking for more, *hoping* for more. And those fond wishes were unlikely to be granted. Nor, to be fair to him, had he ever suggested that there would be more between them than he had originally offered.

Carmela had already packed for the proposed cruise round the Mediterranean and Jazz chatted on the phone to her mother and her aunt, who were all agog and fascinated by the newspaper revelations but wildly overexcited at the prospect of staying on a billionaire's yacht for at least a week.

Back to basics, Jazz told herself firmly as she climbed into the helicopter that had landed in the castle grounds with her mother and her aunt already on board. And the basic bottom line on her marriage with Vitale was that they had married solely to legitimise their unborn children. It shocked Jazz to force herself to remember that modest truth. When had she begun moving so dangerously far from that original agreement? Hadn't she known in her heart even at the beginning that she felt far more for Vitale than she should? In other words, she was suffering from a self-inflicted injury. He had not asked her to love him, had never sought that deeper bond or hinted at more lasting ties. In fact, Vitale had married her while openly talking about divorcing her, so she couldn't blame him for misleading her or lying in any way. No, she could only blame herself for not keeping better control of her emotions.

Angel's yacht, *Siren*, rejoiced in such size and splendour that Jazz's mother and aunt were completely overpowered by the luxury and quite failed to notice Jazz's unusual quietness. Separated from Vitale, she felt horribly alone and empty.

Over the next few days while the trio of women sunbathed, swam and shopped in the island towns the yacht visited, Jazz continued to avidly read online reports of the latest developments in Lerovia. Vitale had been declared King and the popular unrest had subsided almost immediately because he was expected to be a modern rather than traditional monarch as his mother had been described. He phoned Jazz every evening, polite strained calls that did nothing to raise her spirits. The coronation had been scheduled for the following month.

Vitale was free now, Jazz thought unhappily, free for the first time in his life from his mother's demands and interference. But he wasn't free in his marriage, Jazz acknowledged wretchedly, feeling like the final obstacle in his path to full liberation. After all, if she hadn't fallen pregnant he wouldn't have been married to a woman unqualified to become his Queen. But what could he possibly do about it now? He could hardly divorce her while she was still pregnant, so he was stuck with making the best of things until he was free to make a better choice.

Thinking such downbeat thoughts, Jazz studied her changing body shape in the bedroom mirror. Her stomach was developing a rounded curve while her waist was losing definition and her breasts were now overflowing her *new* bras. Shopping for maternity clothing could not be put off much longer but the very idea of such a trip made her feel unattractive.

'I've decided to go home to London with Mum and Clodagh tomorrow,' Jazz informed Vitale when he phoned that evening. 'It would get me out of your hair.'

An abrupt little silence fell on the line.

'What if I don't want you out of my hair?' Vitale demanded with sudden harshness.

'Well, you did say that you were comforted by the idea of me being away from you on this yacht, so I thought that possibly me being in London would have the same effect.'

'It *wouldn't.*' Vitale's voice was cold and clipped and very emphatic in tone.

'Oh… I expect I'm needed for things at the palace,' she muttered ruefully.

'You are,' Vitale confirmed without skipping a beat, wondering what on earth had got into her, and from where she had picked up such strange ideas.

Only slowly and with effort did he register that avoiding talking about the kind of stuff he had always avoided talking about could be the single biggest mistake he had ever made. Silence didn't work on Jazz as it had on his mother. Jazz wasn't content to fill the silence with the sound of her own voice. She would be too busy judging everything he said and did as though it were a crime scene and reaching her own dangerous conclusions.

Vitale got off the phone very quickly after that exchange and it unnerved Jazz, who had assumed that he would encourage her to go to London. She wondered if she would ever understand the conflicting signals he gave her. First, he wanted her, next he didn't want her, then he wanted her again. She supposed the crisis was over now and possibly that was the cause of his change of attitude. Weary of speculating about a man who had always confounded her expectations but whom she would have walked over fire to protect, Jazz dined with her family and then went for a shower.

When the helicopter came in to land, she was wrapped in a towel and seated out on the private terrace off the master suite watching the sun go down in flaming splendour. Having assumed that the craft was merely delivering supplies, she sped indoors again to escape the noise and was completely taken aback when Vitale strode in only minutes later.

'What are you doing here?' Jazz gasped in disconcertion while her eyes travelled with guilt-ridden enthusiasm over his lean, powerful figure, admiring the fit of his jeans over his long, hard thighs and the breadth of his chest below his black shirt. He returned her scrutiny, attention lodging on the edge of the towel biting into the exuberant fullness of her breasts, and she reddened, horribly self-conscious at being caught undressed and without a lick of make-up on.

'I...I missed you,' Vitale declared with unexpected abruptness.

Her green eyes widened. 'You...*did*?'

'Of course, I did. I only sent you away for your benefit and I assumed you'd appreciate a private break with your family,' Vitale asserted almost accusingly. 'I had too much official business to take of at the palace and very little time to spare for you.'

Jazz stiffened at the reminder. 'I understood that.'

'No, you seem to think I wanted to get rid of you and that is not true at all. In fact it is *so* untrue, it's ridiculous!' Vitale informed her on a rising note of unconcealed annoyance. 'If you'd stayed on at the palace you wouldn't have been able to go out those first few days and I was in back-to-back meetings. It would have been selfish to keep you cooped up just for my own pleasure.'

Jazz froze. 'When you sent me away I felt like

I was an annoying distraction to you, just one more burden.'

Vitale stilled by the door that led out to the terrace, his lean, darkly handsome features rigid. 'You are not and have never been a burden. In fact you are the only thing in my life that has ever given me pure pleasure...'

Jazz loved to hear nice things about herself but that was too over-the-top and from Vitale, of all people, to convince her. 'I can't believe that.'

Vitale's hands knotted into fists of frustration and he made a gesture with both arms that telegraphed his inability to explain what he had meant with that statement.

'I'm being snappy because I was hurt when you sent me away,' Jazz admitted guiltily, badly wanting to put her arms round him and only just resisting the temptation by filling the uneasy silence for him.

'Do you think it didn't hurt me to be without you every day?' Vitale shot back at her at startling speed. 'Not even to have a few minutes I could call my own with you? But I was trying to do the right thing, only somehow it seems to have been the wrong thing...the story of my *every* dealing with you!' he completed bitterly.

'Would you like a drink?' she asked uncomfortably.

'No, thanks. I had a couple of drinks after you announced your intention of returning to London and it didn't noticeably improve my mood,' he admitted wearily.

'I thought you might welcome my departure. Clearly I misunderstood,' Jazz said for him, reading between the lines, reckoning that he had flown out to the yacht because he was panicking at the idea that she might run out on their marriage even before the coronation and cause yet another scandal. 'I wasn't threatening to leave you, Vitale.'

'*Per meraviglia*...you *weren't*?' Vitale froze to prompt in open bewilderment and disbelief.

'No, I wouldn't let you down like that. I wouldn't do that to you. As you said, we're in this together. Whatever happens, I'll stick things out at the palace until you think it's the right time for us to separate and go for a divorce,' Jazz promised him earnestly.

Vitale paled below his bronzed complexion, stunning dark golden eyes narrowing as if he was pained by that speech. 'I don't want a divorce any more. I want to stay married to you until the day I die, *amata mia*. I know we didn't start out with that understanding and that I'm ignoring the terms we agreed on but… I've changed.'

'Have you?' Jazz said doubtfully. 'Or is it that you feel us divorcing so soon after your mother's abdication will look bad?'

'You are a very difficult woman to reason with,' Vitale groaned, raking long brown fingers through his already-tousled black hair. 'When I said I changed, I meant *I* changed, nothing to do with the crown or my mother or anyone else. You and I are the only two people in this marriage and I really don't want to lose you. That's why I'm here. I also had to resign from the bank.'

'You've resigned?' Jazz was taken aback.

'Naturally. I can't be a king and a banker as well. I also need time to be a husband and father.

Something had to go to give us enough space for a family life,' he pointed out. 'But if you still want a divorce, of course—'

'I didn't say that!' Jazz interrupted in haste.

'Everything you've said and done implies that, though,' Vitale condemned with curt finality, squaring his broad shoulders as if awaiting a physical blow.

'You take the worst possible meaning out of everything I say,' Jazz scolded without meaning to. 'I'm waiting for you to tell me why you decided you wanted to stay married to me…'

'I answered that,' Vitale contradicted squarely. 'You make me happy…and,' he hesitated before adding with visible discomfiture, 'I love you.'

He said it so quietly and so quickly that she wasn't quite sure she had heard him correctly.

'I mean,' Vitale began afresh with a faint air of desperation, 'I *suppose* it's love. I *hate* it when you're away from me. I miss you so much. I can't imagine being with any other woman. You're different somehow—*special*—and you know how I think—which I didn't like at first—but I'm beginning to believe I should be grateful for that. I know you're not happy at the idea of me becoming King… I *did* see your face when that reality dawned on you but I really don't think I can do it without you,' he told her awkwardly. 'If it came to a choice between the throne and you, I would choose you…'

Jazz's heart expanded like a giant warm globe inside her ribcage as she appreciated that she was listening to a genuine but rather clumsy declaration of love and in a sudden movement she moved closer and wrapped both arms round him. 'I'd never ask you to make a choice like that. I'm not thrilled at the idea of being a queen or being on show all the time, but if I have you with me I'll survive it,' she declared breathlessly, her hands sliding up over his torso and round his neck. 'Why? Because I love you too, you crazy man. How could you miss the fact that I love you?'

Vitale released his pent-up breath in an audible surge and closed both arms tightly round her, a slight shudder of reaction rocking his lean body against her. 'You do?' he pressed uncertainly. 'But why? I'm kind of boring compared to you.'

'No, you're not!' she argued feelingly, hurt that he could think that of himself.

'You're chatty and funny and lively, every-thing I'm not,' Vitale persisted argumentatively. 'It's like you're a magnet. You pulled me in even though I tried very hard to resist you.'

'You didn't resist for very long,' Jazz com-mented, thinking about their encounter in the kitchen on the first night of her stay at his town house.

'You were more temptation than I could resist. Everything about you attracted me.'

'No, you tried to change everything about me to make me presentable,' she reminded him. 'All those lessons.'

'That was educational stuff to ensure that you could hold your own in any company. I live in a different world and I wanted you to feel as comfortable and confident in it as I do. That's past. We've moved way beyond that level now,' he pointed out.

'Yes.' Momentarily, Jazz simply rested her brow against a warm shoulder sheathed in fresh scented cotton and drank in the familiar smell of him. A silly, happy sense of peace was flooding her because Vitale was finally hers, absolutely, irretrievably hers. He had learned to love her in spite of their many differences and perhaps the most wonderful discovery of all was that, mismatched or not, together they made a very comfortable and secure whole.

'But you kept on reminding me that we were supposed to be getting a divorce,' he muttered grimly.

'Well, that is how you set up our marriage,' Jazz reminded him helplessly.

'I know,' Vitale groaned out loud. 'But every time you threw that at me, panic gripped me. I'd dug myself into this ridiculous deep dark hole and I didn't know how to get out of it again. I didn't want to let you go but I'd *promised* you that I would and I always keep my promises. I made such a mess out of everything between us. I should've told you sooner that I no longer wanted a divorce but I was afraid you'd tell me that you still wanted your freedom back and I couldn't face that. In fact I thought it was wiser to keep quiet about my plans.'

'Honesty works best with me…even if I don't want to hear it, and what you *didn't* say,' she told him for future reference, 'was what I most wanted to hear these past few weeks.'

'Why did our royal wedding upset you so much?'

Jazz withdrew her arms and stepped back from him to look at him. *'Seriously?* You're asking me that when *six* suitable wife candidates followed me down the aisle?'

His brow furrowed in bewilderment. 'Suitable wife candidates?'

'From that file of your mother's. Didn't you recognise them? I mean, you must have met at least a couple of them prior to our big day,' she reasoned.

'The bridesmaids were the women in that file?' Vitale demanded, dark colour edging his hard cheekbones as comprehension sank in and he muttered something unrepeatable in Italian. '*Madonna diavolo...* I never looked at those photographs or that file. It's called passive resistance and I refused to encourage my mother's delusions by playing along with them.'

'You never even looked?' Jazz repeated in astonishment.

'No, I refused. Even when she spread the photos on her desk in front of me, I refused to look. But that she asked them to act as your bridesmaids sickens me,' Vitale admitted with a furious shake of his proud dark head. 'It's hard to credit that even she could be that vindictive. You should've told me.'

'I assumed that you would recognise them. Anyway,' Jazz framed uncomfortably, 'reading that file was bad for my confidence. I started making these awful comparisons between me and those women and my self-esteem sank very low and that made me very touchy and more inclined to misinterpret everything you did.'

'Even though you are head and shoulders above the women in that pointless pretentious file?' Vitale demanded. 'Because you are the woman I love and the *only* woman I want as a wife!'

And he *meant* every word of that declaration, Jazz recognised with her self-esteem taking a resulting leap as she accepted that wonderful truth. He thought more of her than she thought of herself, she registered in awe.

'Even though you once said I was as flat as an ironing board?' she began teasingly.

'Not a problem we have now,' Vitale told her with a flashing smile as he unwound the towel and backed her purposefully towards the bed. 'As for the hair—I love your hair and you know I do. I've told you often enough.'

And he was always playing with her hair, she conceded thoughtfully while she allowed herself to be rearranged on the bed, a little tremor of awareness and hunger sliding through her as Vitale lowered his long, lean, powerful body down over hers. 'I love you,' he said again. 'And I haven't slept a night through since you left me. I miss the hugs.'

'Well, you have to start hugging back to get

them,' Jazz informed him with dancing eyes of challenge.

And he hugged her and she giggled like a drain. 'Again!' she demanded like a child.

The happiness Jazz had brought into his life far outweighed every other concern, Vitale appreciated, and his answering smile was brilliant.

'Oh, I do love you, Vitale,' she whispered when she could breathe again, because he was a little too enthusiastic with his hugs. 'When did you realise how you felt about me?'

'I should've realised the day I almost punched Angel for flirting with you because I was jealous.'

'You *were*.' Jazz savoured that belated admission with unhidden satisfaction.

'But it took me a lot longer to realise what you'd done to me.'

'What I'd done to you?' Jazz queried.

'*Sì*...turned me upside down, inside out and head over heels and all without me having a clue about what was happening,' Vitale confided ruefully. 'And then you never missed a chance to remind me about the divorce plan. That was a real own goal on my part.'

Jazz smiled. 'Glad you recognise that.'

Vitale rubbed his jawline gently over her smooth cheek. 'I shaved... Do I have to keep on talking all night?'

Jazz laughed, feeling amazingly cheerful. 'No, you don't have to talk any more.'

'*Grazie a Dio*,' Vitale's sigh of relief was heartfelt. He realised that he was much more like his emotional father than he had ever appreciated, although he still lacked his father's ability to easily discuss his feelings. But the key to his happiness was Jazz, he acknowledged. Jazz, who had taught him how to enjoy life again. He could cope with anything as long as she was by his side.

And Jazz looked up at him with eyes that shone with love and appreciation and, eagerly drinking in that appraisal, Vitale kissed her with all the passion she inspired in him. They made love and the rest of the world was forgotten. Later, much, much later, she twitted him about the prenup agreement that had so depressed her and he kissed her again, contriving to avoid talking once more with remarkable efficiency, but then when Vitale learned anything to his advantage he was always quick to use it.

EPILOGUE

FIVE YEARS LATER Jazz lay back on her sun lounger in the shade and watched the children play in the new swimming pool. Angel was on duty as a lifeguard and, considering that a good half of the overexcited children belonged to him and Merry, that was only fair. Jazz had had to nag at Vitale to get him to agree to a pool at the Italian farmhouse because he liked their lifestyle there to be simpler and less luxurious than life in Lerovia.

'Enrico!' her husband suddenly yelled full throttle at the four-year-old trying to push his twin brother into the pool. 'Stop it!'

Enrico grinned, mischief dancing in his dark eyes, and while he wasn't looking his twin, Donato, gave him a crafty shove into the water.

'That was dangerous!' Vitale thundered.

'The men get so het up when the kids are only

doing what comes naturally,' Merry marvelled from her seat beside Jazz while her own little tribe frolicked in the water, noisily jumping up and down and splashing each other.

'But then they're not as accustomed as we are to the daily shenanigans.' Jazz sighed, smoothing her light dress down over the prominent swell of her abdomen.

'Are you hoping for a girl this time around?' Merry asked with the casual curiosity of a close friend.

'I think Vitale is but I don't care as long as the baby's healthy,' Jazz confided, thinking how worried and stressed she had been when her newly born twins had had to go straight into incubators after their premature birth.

Enrico and Donato had thrived from that point on and had soon gained sufficient strength to take up residence in the colourful nursery their parents had created for them at the palace. But, still, Jazz would not have liked to go through the experience of having to leave her babies in hospital again while she went home alone. Her current pregnancy, however, had been much easier than the first. She had been less sick and she felt much more relaxed about her condition, although, if anything, Vitale fussed even more than he had the first time around.

Their lives in Lerovia had gone through a dizzying cycle of change in every sphere. First of all, they had had to move into what had previously been Vitale's mother's wing of the palace. A full-scale redecoration had been required and Jazz still sometimes suspected that she could smell wet paint. Vitale had opened up the ceremonial rooms of the palace to the public for the first time and now Jazz's mother was happily engaged in running the palace gift shop and café opened in a rear courtyard.

Peggy Dickens had made a new life in Lerovia. She had wanted to be close to her grandchildren and she now occupied a small palace apartment where her sister, Clodagh, was a regular guest. Jazz had been relieved when her mother had passed her most recent health check with flying colours and she was delighted to have her only parent living within easy reach. Vitale had been very generous agreeing to that development, she thought fondly. Not every man would have wanted his mother-in-law living on his doorstep. He had been equally generous when Peggy had told him that she wanted to get involved with the huge challenge of opening part of the palace to the public. Able to engage in meaningful work again, Peggy had gone from strength to strength and had rediscovered her vitality and interest in life.

When the twins were a few months old, Jazz had completed her degree in the History of Art at the University of Leburg and had graduated with honours. Now she was one of the directors of the Leburg Art museum and all the paintings in the palace had finally been exhaustively catalogued, which had led to the exciting discovery of an Old Master of one of Vitale's ancestors. Her life was incredibly busy but she loved it.

The tiny country of Lerovia had become her home and she was a very popular working royal. Prince Eduardo now regularly conducted public engagements on his nephew's behalf and was fully restored to the status his sister had once taken from him. Jazz had been shocked when Vitale had informed her that it had been Eduardo who had choreographed Queen Sofia's downfall by tipping off a friend in the media about her affair.

'It was payback for a lifetime of slights. Mean and cruel of him,' Vitale had conceded of his uncle's behaviour. 'But who am I to criticise? Eduardo was once a very popular member of the family and my mother cut him out of our lives and kept him criminally short of money. He didn't deserve that and her mistreatment of her brother came back to haunt her.'

Sofia Castiglione, now known as Princess Sofia, was still living in her opulent Alpine chalet with Cinzia. She phoned Vitale from time to time to reprimand him about changes she had heard he was instigating and she warned him that he would lose the respect of the people if he lessened the mystique of the monarchy by embracing a less luxurious lifestyle. She had flatly refused to ever set foot in Lerovia again, confessing that she had never liked the Lerovians, and Vitale had laughed heartily when he'd shared that particular gem with Jazz. He had visited his mother on several occasions but he did it out of duty, rather than affection. His failure to divorce Jazz had infuriated his mother and Jazz was still waiting, but not with bated breath, for an invitation to the Alpine chalet.

Charles Russell, on the other hand, was a regular visitor, particularly when the family were vacationing at the farmhouse where he too enjoyed relaxing. He was a great grandparent, always ready to put his book down to enter the world of small children and entertain them.

After dinner that evening, Jazz stepped gratefully into the candlelit bath awaiting her and smiled widely when Vitale brought her lemonade in a wine glass.

'You're not supposed to climb in until I'm here in case you fall,' Vitale censured, his lean, darkly handsome face full of concern.

'I'm not as big as I was with the twins,' Jazz murmured softly. 'I'm not going to fall.'

Vitale smoothed a coiling ringlet back from her damp brow. 'Naked in candlelight you look incredibly sexy, *bellezza mia…*'

'Don't call me beautiful like this,' Jazz scolded with a slight grimace down at the swell of her stomach. 'Or sexy.'

'But it's the truth.' Vitale levelled stunning dark golden eyes on her and smiled again. 'You want me to lie?'

'Oh, for goodness' sake,' she muttered, passing him her empty glass and rising to leave the bath.

Vitale wrapped her in a fleecy towel and scooped her out.

'You're getting wet!' she cried crossly.

Vitale grinned wickedly down at her. 'I won't be keeping my wet clothes on for long.'

Jazz rolled her beautiful green eyes. 'Now there's confidence for you,' she teased as he carried her back into their bedroom, a big airy space with a cosy corner by the fire for their winter visits.

'Am I wrong?' Vitale husked, pressing a kiss to the pulse point at her throat, sending her body haywire with response.

'Sadly, no. I'm always a pushover,' she sighed, finding his beautiful mouth again for herself and exulting in the love he gave her so freely and the happiness they had found together against all the odds.

* * * * *